THE BACKSTABBER MAKES HIS MOVE

Out where war mecha jousted with spears of pure annihilation for the fate of the super dimensional fortress and the human race, lines of ferociously intense fire crisscrossed, taking a heavy toll on both sides.

Despite a steady rain of energy blasts from the SDF-1's primary and secondary batteries, Khyron's cruiser swung in a low pass toward the battle fortress. The SDF-1's fire was punishing his ship, but that didn't matter to Khyron the Backstabber; the alien's cruiser passed overhead, all turrets firing, as the two heavyweight ships hammered away at each other, inflicting appalling damage.

Then Khyron's cruiser released a virtual hail of Battlepods that dropped down toward the SDF-1, the pods and the tri-thruster pursuit ships keeping up a heavy fusillade. The VTs did their best to turn back the assault-drop, but were simply outnumbered. There would be many empty bunks in the squadrons' quarters that night.

If indeed the SDF-1 lasted through the day...

Published by Ballantine Books:

THE ROBOTECH™ SERIES

THE SENTINELS™ SERIES

ROBOTECH™ #3:

HOMECOMING

Jack McKinney

A Del Rey® Book
BALLANTINE BOOKS • NEW YORK

A Del Rey® Book
Published by Ballantine Books
Copyright © 1987 by HARMONY GOLD U.S.A. INC. and TATSUNOKO PRODUCTION CO., LTD.

All rights reserved under International and Pan-American Copyright Conventions. Published in the United States by Ballantine Books, a division of Random House, Inc., New York, and simultaneously in Canada by Random House of Canada Limited, Toronto.

Cover art by David Schleinkofer

Library of Congress Catalog Card Number: 86-91634

ISBN 0-345-34136-8

Printed in Canada

First Edition: March 1987

23 22 21 20 19 18 17 16 15 14

FOR RISA KESSLER,
WITH THANKS AND HIGH REGARD

CHAPTER
ONE

The enemy armada, so vastly superior to us in numbers of fighting mecha and aggregate firepower, continues to harry and harass us. But time and again the Zentraedi stop short of all-out attack. They impede our long voyage back to Earth, but they cannot stop us. I am still uncertain as to what good fortune is working in the SDF-1's favor.

I do not point out any of this to the crew or refugees, however. It does no good to tell grieving friends and loved ones that casualties could have been far worse.

From the log of Captain Henry Gloval

BLUE LINES OF ENEMY CANNON FIRE STREAKED BY Roy Fokker's cockpit, scorching one of his Veritech fighter's tail stabilizers, ranging in for a final volley.

"Flying sense" the aviators called it, jargon that came from the twentieth-century term "air sense": honed and superior high-speed piloting instincts. It was something a raw beginner took a while to develop, something that separated the novices from the vets.

And it was something Lieutenant Commander Roy Fokker, Skull Team leader and Veritech squadron commander, had in abundance, even in the airlessness of a deep-space dogfight.

Responding to his deft touch at the controls and his very will—passed along to it by Robotech sensors in his flight helmet—Roy's Veritech fighter did a wingover and veered onto a new vector with tooth-snapping force.

1

Thrusters blaring full-bore, the maneuver forces pressed him into his seat, just as the enemy was concentrating more on his aim than on his flying.

The Zentraedi in the Battlepod on Roy's tail, trying so diligently to kill him and destroy his Robotech fighter, was a good pilot, steady and cool like all of them, but he lacked Roy's flying abilities.

While the giant alien gaped, astounded, at his suddenly empty gunsight reticle, the Skull Team leader was already coming around behind the pod into the kill position.

Around that fragment of the battle, an enormous dogfight raged as Zentraedi pods and their Cyclops recon ships mixed it up ferociously with the grimly determined human defenders in their Veritechs. The bright spherical explosions characteristic of zero-g battle blossomed all around, dozens at a time. Blue Zentraedi radiation blasts were matched by the Veritechs' autocannons, which flung torrents of high-density armor-piercers at the enemy.

Roy was relieved to see that the SDF-1 was unharmed. Most of the fighting seemed to be going on at some distance from it, although it was clear that the enemy fleet had all the odds on its side. The Zentraedi armada easily numbered over a million warships.

Roy located his wingman, Captain Kramer, in the furious engagement; forming up for mutual security, he looked around again for the fantastic Zentraedi mecha that had done so much damage a few minutes before. It had flown rings around the Veritechs that had gone after it, taking Roy and the Skulls by surprise and smashing their formation after cutting a swath through Vermilion Team.

Whatever it was, it was unlike any Zentraedi weapon the humans had seen so far. Unlike the pods, which resembled towering metal ostriches bristling with guns, the newcomer was more human-shaped—a bigger, more hulking, and heavily armed and armored version of the

Veritechs' own Battloid mode. And fast—frightfully fast and impossible to stop, eluding even the SDF-1's massive defensive barrages.

Roy had expected to see the battle fortress under intense attack; instead, the super dimensional fortress was cruising along unbothered and alone. Moreover, transmissions over the tac net indicated that the Zentraedi pods and Cyclopses were withdrawing. Roy couldn't figure that out.

He switched from the tac net to SDF-1's command net. There was word of the new Zentraedi mecha. The thing had made it as far as SDF-1—getting in beneath the fields of fire of most of the ship's batteries—then had suddenly withdrawn at blinding speed, outmaneuvering gunfire and outracing pursuit. The ship had suffered only minor damage, and the operations and intelligence people had concluded that the whole thing had been a probing attack of some kind, a test of a new machine and new tactics.

Roy didn't care as long as the battle fortress was still safe. He gathered the Veritechs, ready to head home.

"Enemy pod," Skull Five called over the tac net. "Bearing one-niner-four-seven."

Roy already had the computer reference on one of his situation screens. A pod, all right, but evidently damaged and drifting, none of its weapons firing; it was leaking atmosphere.

"Could be a trick," Skull Seven said. "What d' ya think, skipper? Do we blast it out of the sky?"

"Negative; somebody may still be alive in there, and a live captive is what the intelligence staff's been praying for." The incredible savagery of this deep-space war was such that few survived as casualties. Alien or human, a fighter almost always either triumphed or died, a simple formula. The humans had never recovered a living enemy.

Besides, for very personal reasons, Roy was especially eager to see a Zentraedi undergo interrogation.

"We're getting signals from it, nothing we can un-scramble," a communications officer reported over the command net.

Whatever was going on, none of the Zentraedi forces seemed to be turning back for a rescue. Veritech fly-bys drew no fire; eyeball inspection and instruments indicated that the damaged pod's main power source had been knocked out but that some of its weapons were still functioning. Nevertheless, it passed up several opportunities to blast away at nearby VTs.

"This is too good an opportunity to pass up," Gloval finally announced over the main command net. "If there is a survivor aboard, we must get him into the SDF-1 immediately."

"That thing could be booby-trapped—or its occupant could be!" a security staff officer protested from one of Roy's display screens.

Gloval replied, "That is why we will push the pod closer to SDF-1—but not too close—and connect a boarding tube to it. An EVA team will make a thorough examination before we permit it any closer."

"But—" the officer began.

Roy cut in over the command net, "You heard the captain, so put a sock in it, mac!" Roy was elated with Gloval's decision; it was only a slim hope, but now there *was* hope of finding out what had happened to Roy's closest friend in the world, Rick Hunter and Lisa Hayes and the others who'd disappeared on their desperate mission to guide the SDF-1 through danger.

Roy began swinging into place, shifting his ship to Battloid mode. "Okay, Skull Team; time to play a little bumper cars."

Two more Skulls went to Battloid, their Robotech ships transforming and reconfiguring. When the shift was complete, the war machines looked like enormous armored ultramech knights.

They joined Roy in pushing the inert pod back toward the battle fortress.

* * *

The men and women of the EVA—Extra Vehicular Activity—crews were efficient and careful. *They're also gutsy as hell*, Roy reflected, his Battloid towering over them in the boarding tube lock. But of course, everybody knew and honored the legendary dedication and tenacity of the EVA crews.

Crowded into the boarding tube lock with two other Battloids behind him, Roy watched expectantly. The huge lock, extending from the SDF-1 at the end of nearly a mile of large-diameter tube, was a yawning dome on a heavy base, equipped with every sort of contingency gear imaginable. The captured pod and EVA crew and Roy's security detail took up only a small part of its floor space.

"Not beat up too bad," the EVA crew chief observed over the com net. "But I dunno how much air it lost. What d' ya say, Fokker? Do we open 'er up?" She was holding a thermotorch ready. She'd turned to gaze up at Roy's cockpit.

As ranking officer on the scene, Lt. Comdr. Roy Fokker had the responsibility of advising Gloval. Tampering with the pod was very risky; they could trigger some kind of booby trap humans couldn't even imagine, destroying everyone there and perhaps even damaging the SDF-1.

But we can't go on fighting war this way! Roy thought. *Knowing next to nothing about these creatures we're up against or even why we're fighting—we can't go on like this much longer!*

"Cap'n Gloval, sir, I say we take a shot."

"Very well. Good luck to you," Gloval answered. "Proceed."

Roy reached down and put a giant hand in front of the EVA crew chief, blocking her way as she approached the enemy mecha. "Sorry, Pietra; this is my party."

His Battloid stood upright again and walked to the pod, shouldering its autocannon, its footsteps shaking the deck. "Cover me," he told his teammates, and they fanned out, muzzles leveled, for clear fields of fire. The Battloid's forearms extruded metal tentacles, complicated waldos and manipulators, and thermotorches.

"Just try not to break anything unnecessarily," Pietra warned, and led her crew to the shelter of a blast shield.

Roy looked the pod over, trying a few external controls tentatively. Nothing happened. He moved closer still, examining the pressure seals that ran around the great hatch at the rear top of the pod's bulbous torso. Being this close to a pod's guns had him sweating under his VT helmet.

"Careful, Roy," Kramer said quietly.

He didn't want to use the torch for fear of fire or explosion. He decided to try simply pulling the pod's hatch open with the Battloid's huge, strong hands. He ran his ship's fingers along the seams, feeling for a place to grab hold . . .

The pod shook, rattled, and began to open.

Roy's Battloid leapt back, weapon aimed, as the hatch lifted up. Battloid forefingers tightened on triggers, but there was no occupant immediately to be seen.

However, the Battloids' external sound sensors relayed a remarkable exchange, muffled and a little resonant, coming from the pod.

"Well, finally! Thank goodness! When you start bragging to your fighter pilot buddies about *this* mission, boys, don't forget it took you just about forever to get a simple hatch open!"

That voice was womanly and very pleasant, if a little arch and teasing. Another, a young male's, sounding highly insulted, answered, "You weren't so hot at getting in touch with your precious bridge, I noticed!"

If this is some kind of trick, we're up against the zaniest enemies in the universe, Roy thought.

"I thought you both did very well," another male voice said calmly, humbly—placatingly.

"Ah, look out, Max," the first male voice said. "And let's get outta here."

There was a certain amount of grunting and straining then, and at one point the female voice yelled, "Ben, if you don't get your big foot out of my face, I'm going to break it off!" A vociferous argument broke out.

"Everybody shut up!" the first male voice screamed. "Ben, Max: Gimme a boost up, here."

Moments later, two flight-gloved, human-size hands gripped the edge of the hatch. A dark mop of black hair rose into view.

Rick Hunter, standing on the head of the husky Ben Dixon, hauled himself up triumphantly.

"Hold your fire! We're back! Roy, we escaped from the Zentraedi—um . . ."

Three Battloids stood there looking at him, hands resting casually on the upturned muzzles of their grounded autocannon, heads cocked to one side or the other. Their attitude seemed to be one of resigned disgust.

"We escaped!" Rick repeated, thinking perhaps they hadn't heard him. "Man, have we got stories to tell! We were in an enemy ship! We met their leaders! We shot our way out in this pod! We . . . we . . . What's wrong?"

Roy couldn't tell Rick how overjoyed and relieved he was; it would have spoiled their friendship.

"We were *hoping* for a POW," he said. "Boy, is Captain Gloval gonna be sore at you for not being a Zentraedi."

CHAPTER TWO

The Zentraedi version of psychology could only be termed primitive, of course, except as it applied to such things as maintaining military discipline and motivating warriors. And even there, it was brutal and straightforward.

No surprise, then, that when those particular three Zentraedi were quick to accept their spying mission, Breetai scarcely thought twice about it.

But of course, he hadn't spent as much time watching transmissions of the swimsuit portion of the Miss Macross contest.

Zeitgeist, *Alien Psychology*

THE SDF-1'S SURVIVAL OF THE LATEST ZENTRAEDI attack had buoyed morale all through the ship—at least in most cases; there were those whom the lessons of war had made too wary to quickly believe in good fortune. Even with Earth looming large before it and the long, dark billions of miles safely crossed, the battle fortress was dogged by the enemy—now more than ever. Continued vigilance was imperative.

One of those acutely aware of the continuing danger was Claudia Grant, who was acting as the vessel's First Officer in Lisa Hayes's absence. Though Claudia and Lisa were friends, Claudia had always felt a little put off by Lisa's single-minded devotion to duty, her severity. But now, elevated to the responsibilities of her new position—especially at this moment, with Gloval off the bridge—Claudia was seeing things in a different light.

The members of her usual watch, the female enlisted-rating techs, Sammie, Kim, and Vanessa, were off duty for a long-postponed pass into Macross City. Lisa, Claudia, and the other three had formed something very much like a family, with Gloval as patriarch; they had become a highly efficient team both under everyday stresses and demands and under fire.

The turmoil of the war had brought an assortment of other techs to the bridge on relief watches, and Claudia didn't trust any of them to really know what they were doing, just as Lisa hadn't. So even though she was almost out on her feet with fatigue, Claudia had refused to be relieved of her duties as long as Gloval was away.

There was no telling how long that would be. The glorious news of the rescue of Lisa and the others was tarnished by the fact that the SDF-1 was still surrounded by the enemy armada. Debriefings and command conferences might go on for a very long while.

Claudia looked up wearily from her instruments as she heard one of the relief-watch techs say wistfully, "Boy, is that beautiful! D' you think we'll ever set foot on Earth again?"

The tech had brought up a long-range image of their blue-white homeworld on the screen before her.

Claudia was a tall woman in her late twenties, with exotic good looks and glowing honey-brown skin. Her dark eyes twinkled and shone when she was happy, and flashed when she was angry. Right now, they were flashing like warning beacons.

"Why don't you go ask the commander of that Zentraedi fleet? Go ahead, take a look at them! Maybe they've gone away!"

The tech, a teenage girl who wore her auburn hair in a pageboy and still didn't look quite comfortable in uniform, swallowed and went a little pale. Claudia Grant's temper was well known, and she had the size and speed to back it up when she needed to.

The tech worked her controls obediently, bringing up a visual of the Zentraedi fleet. They were all around the battle fortress, standing out of range of the ship's secondary batteries and lesser weapons. They were like a seaful of predatory fish—cruisers and destroyers and smaller craft in swarms, blocking out the stars. And farther away, the instruments registered their flagship: *nine miles* of armor and heavy weapons.

The tech gasped, eyes big and round.

"Still there, huh?" Claudia nodded, knowing full well they were. "All right, then, let's not hear any more about wanting to go home; not until our job's done. Understood?"

The tech hastened to say, "Aye aye!" as did the rest of the watch.

Claudia eased off a bit, looking around at the watch members. "There are a lot of folks depending on us. And I guarantee you, you *don't* want to know what it feels like to let people down in a situation like this."

In a far-off compartment of the SDF-1, three strange beings skulked and crept around. They were not Zentraedi, at least not any longer; they were of human scale. But neither could they fairly be called human, though that was the appearance they gave; until a few hours before they had been members of the giant warrior race.

The devastatingly fast and ferocious enemy mecha that had wreaked such havoc among the VTs—the one the humans hadn't seen before—had put this threesome aboard. The one thing they *could* accurately be called was "spies."

They had hastily retreated from the metal canister in which they'd arrived. The mighty Quadrono Battalion mecha that had, in its lightning raid, torn open a section of the SDF-1's hull to toss them inside had also (understandably enough) attracted a certain amount of attention. If the canister was found before it quietly dissolved, it might set off a massive search.

The smallest of the three, Rico, said, "Okay, let's start spying!" He was dark-haired and wiry.

The sturdy Bron, a head taller, said sourly, "But we can't spy in these clothes; they'll know who we are!"

Even though the Zentraedi military had little experience in espionage—out-and-out battle was what the warrior race preferred—it was obvious that Bron was right. The Zentraedi fleet carried no wardrobe in human size, of course, and so the three wore improvised, shapeless knee-length robes of coarsely woven blue sackcloth. The sleeveless robes were gathered at the waist with a turn or two of Zentraedi string, more or less the thickness of clothesline. Not surprisingly, the spies were barefoot.

It all had them a bit shaken, this matter of dress. The Zentraedi drew much of their sense of self from their uniforms. The best the trio had been able to do was agree to maintain the attitude that they were wearing the special attire of an elite unit. A very *small* elite unit.

Konda, nearly Bron's height but lean and angular, shook his hair back out of his eyes. His hair was purple, but intelligence reported that the color wouldn't stand out much in light of current human fads. "Then, let's find some other clothes," Konda proposed.

They'd been given some briefings and rather broad guidelines by Zentraedi intelligence officers, but to a great extent they were improvising as they went along. Still, Konda's idea made a lot of sense. The spies leapt from hiding and set off down a passageway, slipping among the shadows and peering around corners, much more conspicuous than if they'd simply strolled along chatting.

Naturally, SDF-1 had no internal security measures against Zentraedi spies, since it was generally assumed that a fifty-foot-high armored warrior wouldn't be difficult to spot in the average crowd.

There followed a period of ducking and darting, of peeping into various compartments and avoiding any contact with the occasional passerby. The spies knew the general location of the battle fortress's bridge and worked their way in that direction, since the ship's nerve center was something the Zentraedi wanted very much to know about.

As the motley trio peeked out from concealment, they heard a very strange and appealing sound, something none of them had ever heard before. It was human; Konda wondered if it was some alien form of singing, even if it didn't sound very military.

The sound was coming in their direction. They yanked themselves back out of sight. The oddly interesting sound stopped, and the spies heard human female voices.

"Where d' you want to go tonight, Sammie?"

There was the sound of slender shoe heels clicking along the deck. The human females were coming their way, so the spies drew back even deeper into darkness.

"Oh, I don't really care, as long as I can get out of this uniform," Sammie answered.

"Mine feels like it'll be glad to get off me!" Vanessa said.

The Terrible Trio giggled together again; they'd been laughing with delight ever since the relief watch had shown up on the bridge to give them a brief taste of freedom. The hatch to a complex of enlisted ratings' quarters compartments slid open for them and they entered. The hatch closed, shutting off the giggles.

The accelerated course in human language the three spies had been given let them understand the words perfectly, but the content was another question entirely. "What did all that mean?" Konda wondered, rubbing feet that had been made very, very cold by the deck plates.

Little Rico was thinking of a uniform wanting to get off somebody. *Can these creatures have sentient clothing? Perhaps with artificial enhancements? That would indicate a supreme control of Protoculture!* "It seems these Micronians have some great powers."

"Micronians" had always been a derogatory Zentraedi term for small humanoid beings such as *Homo sapiens.* Now, the spies weren't so sure that the condescension was justified.

Bron nodded. "Well, let's keep watch and see what else we can find out."

It seemed like a very long time before the hatch reopened. The Terrible Trio emerged, each dressed for a night on the town in a different, fetching outfit. They laughed and joked, going off in the opposite direction, leaving the very faint but heady fragrance of three perfumes in the passageway.

"Different clothes!" Rico exclaimed softly. *With different powers, perhaps, specialized for a particular mission?*

"I *know*!" Bron said with a certain surprising emphasis.

"Do these people change uniforms every time they do something?" Konda posed a tactical question.

But why, then, did the clothes all look different? The spies somehow knew what they'd just seen weren't uniforms. But how could the Micronians bear to lose their identity by not wearing their uniforms? It was all too unsettling for words.

Not to mention the fact that the three Micronian females looked and sounded, well, somehow delightful. Beguiling. It was very puzzling. The three looked at one another.

"Incredible," Bron summarized.

"Uh, but what does it all mean?" Rico said with troubled brow.

Konda rubbed his jaw in thought. "They changed their clothes in that compartment down there. So that means . . . *we can get disguises!*"

"Good thinking!" Bron cried.

"Let's go!" Rico exploded.

They dashed down the passageway, bare feet slapping the deck. After first making sure nobody was still inside, they piled through the hatch together, anxious to blend in with the Micronians. And though none of them admitted it to the others, they were all thinking of those three intriguing Micronian females but trying not to.

They'd had a previous close encounter with the human enemy, monitoring SDF-1 transmissions that were confusing and puzzling but ever so fascinating. What they'd seen was the swimsuit competition of the ship's Miss Macross pageant. Though they hadn't been able to make head or tail of it, and neither had Zentraedi intelligence analysts, the experience had made Rico, Bron, and Konda eager to sign up for the spying mission.

Inside, various small subcompartments opened off a narrow central passageway. The spies began searching through them, looking for garments that might fit.

They approached the clothes tentatively, timidly. The human fabric constructions *seemed* unthreatening enough, hanging there docilely; but if they somehow incorporated Protoculture forces, there might be no limit to what they could do. The threesome moved as carefully as if they were in the midst of a pack of sleeping Dobermans.

When at last they worked up the nerve to actually touch a dangling cuff and nothing catastrophic happened, the Zentraedi proceeded with more confidence.

A pattern emerged: The lockers in those quarters on the forward side of the passageway tended to have rather recognizable clothing suited to normal activities, even if the cut was a little strange. The ones on the aft side, however, had frilly things, as well as trousers and the skirt-type uniforms the females had worn, as well as more elaborate designs of the same undivided lower garments.

After a lot of rummaging and trying on, Konda and Rico, now in human attire, stepped back into the main passageway. Konda wore dark slacks and a yellow turtleneck, settling the collar uncomfortably. Rico had found blue trousers and a red pullover.

"Hey, Bron, let's get moving!" Rico called.

"This uniform is very unusual," Bron said, lumbering to catch up. "But it's all I can find that fits me. I dressed to conform with a two-dimensional image I saw in that compartment. What d' you think?"

Bron held out the hem of his pleated skirt, standing awkwardly in the large pumps he'd found. His white silk blouse was arranged correctly, its fluffy bow tie and the tasteful string of pearls exactly corresponding to the fashion photo he'd seen.

"Y' look fine, Bron! Now, let's get started," Rico snapped. Bron looked wounded.

Rico was edgy; he and the others had come aboard unarmed, since all Zentraedi weapons were now far too big for them to handle or hide. They'd found no Micronian weapons at all in the humans' personal quarters except those of a makeshift and unsuitable sort. How could these creatures feel any peace of mind without at least a few small arms close at hand? It all made less and less sense.

Bron glowered, and Rico subsided; it was unwise to get the big fellow irritated. Bron gave his skirt a final hitch and said, "Ready."

They fell in together and trooped off in the direction the Terrible Trio had gone, ready to bring triumph and glory to the mighty Zentraedi race.

CHAPTER
THREE

*We had met the enemy, and he wasn't us. Then we wound
up in front of some of "us," and they were the enemy.*

Lisa Hayes, *Recollections*

"**P**LEASE CONTINUE YOUR REPORT, COM-
mander Hayes," the captain bade her.

They sat in high-back chairs along the gleaming conference room table, all in a row. A short time ago they'd
been greeted as heroes, but now—despite Captain Gloval's comforting presence—Lisa felt very much as if she
were sitting before a board of inquiry.

Lisa, Rick, Ben, and Max looked across the long,
wide table at the row of four member officers of the evaluation team. Only one of them held rank in one of the
combat arms, Colonel Maistroff, an Air Group officer
with a reputation as a martinet and stuffed shirt.

The others were intelligence and operations staffers,
though the bearded and balding Major Aldershot was
supposed to be something of a mainstay over at G3
Operations and had earned a Combat Infantry Star in his

youth. The team studied the escapees as if they were something on a microscope slide.

Gloval, presiding at the head of the table, was encouraging Lisa. "You are certain that what you've made is a fair estimate? At this Zentraedi central base there are *really* that many more ships than we've already seen?" The comlink handset next to him began beeping softly; he ignored it.

Lisa thought carefully. So many things about their captivity in the planetoid-size enemy base, a spacefold jump away—somewhere else in the universe—were astounding and unnerving that she rechecked her recollections again, minutely.

Rick looked over to her, and their eyes met. He didn't nod; that might have tainted her testimony. But she saw that he was ready to back her up.

"Yes, sir, at least that many. And quite possibly millions more. I made a conservative estimate."

Gloval, hand on the phone, looked to Rick. "Truly?"

Rick nodded. "Yes, sir. That many."

Gloval listened to the handset for a moment, then replaced it in its cradle without responding. "Based on all combined reports," he resumed, "our computers place the total enemy resources at somewhere between four and five million ships."

"Sir, forgive me, but that's ridiculous," one team member said. From the security branch, he was the officer who'd been all for destroying the escapees' pod. "*Our* projections are based on the most accurate data and statistical techniques known.

"No species could accumulate that sort of power! And even if they could, they couldn't possibly remain at the primitive social and psychological level of these aliens!"

"Now, granted, we're seeing a great deal of military display here," the intel man, a portly fellow in his early thirties, added. "But how many of those ships have actually proved themselves to be combat-ready? A comparative handful! No, Captain; I think what we're seeing is just a bluff. And I think your people here have been taken in by it. My analysis is that Commander Hayes and her party were *permitted* to escape so that they could bring us this...hysterical report and demoralize us."

"Permitted?" Ben Dixon was halfway out of his chair, the big hands clenched into fists, about to leap across the table and pummel the intel officer. "D' you know how many times we almost got killed? How close we came to not making it? When was the last time *you* saw any action, you—"

"Captain!" the intelligence officer burst out to Gloval by way of complaint.

"That will do!" Gloval thundered, and there was sudden silence as Max Sterling and Rick Hunter pulled Ben back.

Having shown his Jovian side for an instant, Gloval lapsed back into a reasonable voice. "Gentlemen, let's hear the entire report before discussing it." It wasn't a suggestion, and everybody understood that. The debriefing team subsided.

Lisa had thought her words out carefully. "In the course of our captivity, we observed that the aliens have absolutely no concept of human emotions. They've been groomed entirely for war. And their society is organized along purely military lines.

"It appears that they've increased their physical size and strength artificially through genetic manipulation and that they also have the ability to reverse the process."

The others present were studying the few video records she'd managed to make surreptitiously during captivity, but Lisa's memory, with Rick's, Ben's, and Max's, provided vivid and chilling recollections. They'd witnessed Zentraedi trans-vid records of the destruction of an entire planet, seen the gigantic protoculture sizing chambers the aliens used to manipulate their size and structure, felt the deathly squeeze of Commander in Chief Dolza's fist around them.

And something else had happened, something Lisa could only bring herself to refer to obliquely. The enemy leaders had been repulsed, but fascinated, by the human custom of kissing. At their demand, and to ascertain what effect it would have on them, Lisa and Rick had kissed, long and deeply, on an enemy conference table as big as a playing field.

None of the four escapees had mentioned the kiss. Lisa still wasn't sure exactly what it was she'd felt afterward. She suspected that Rick was also a little confused, in spite of his love affair with the girl called Minmei. Max and Ben had kept silent, Rick's friends as well as his wingmates.

Lisa finished, "And I think this last part is very important: While they examined and interrogated us, they constantly made reference to something they called 'Protoculture.'"

The intel officer who had almost been attacked by Ben Dixon tilted his chair back arrogantly. "That's pure fantasy."

His security buddy added, "And were there any little green men?"

Major Aldershot glanced around at him stiffly, the ends of his waxed mustache seeming to bristle. "I will point out that the commander is a much-decorated soldier. This insulting levity is unbecoming from someone who has yet to prove himself under fire." It was the most he'd said all morning.

"What is this 'Protoculture'?" Gloval put things back on track.

Lisa hesitated before answering. "It's apparently something that relates to their use of Robotech. I'm not sure, but they think that Protoculture is the highest science in the universe and that somehow *we* possess some of its deepest secrets."

Colonel Maistroff said with a sly grin to the other

evaluation team officers, "Too deep for me!" and guf-
fawed at his own joke.

The intel and security officers roared spitefully along
with him as Lisa's cheeks colored and Rick felt himself
flush in anger.

"Silence!" Gloval barked. It was instantly quiet. "This
is a very grave moment. This alien armada has pursued
and harried us across the solar system for almost a year
and yet has never made an all-out attempt to destroy us;
perhaps we *do* possess a power in the SDF-1 that we
don't fully understand."

That was a good bet, the way Rick saw it. Even the
brilliant Dr. Lang understood only a fraction of the alien
ship's secrets, and he was the one who had master-
minded its reconstruction from a burned and battered
wreck.

Maistroff fixed Lisa with a gimlet stare, red-faced at
being rebuked in front of junior officers. "Commander
Hayes, is that all?"

Lisa met his glare. "Yes, sir, that's all."

Ben whispered to Rick, "I don't think they believe
us." Ben wasn't exactly point man on the genius roster,
and the idea that such a thing could happen had never
occurred to him until the debriefing was well along.

"It's probably the dishonest expression on your face,"
Rick whispered back absently.

Maistroff placed both hands flat on the table and
turned to Gloval. "Do you really believe this wild tale?
It's enemy trickery! Hallucinations!"

Gloval began stoking up his evil-smelling briar, tamp-
ing the tobacco slowly with his thumb, pondering. "This
information must be correlated and reported to Earth immediately, whether I believe it or not—"

Maistroff interrupted him, saying tightly and too
quickly, "I'll send a coded message right away—"

"—Colonel Maistroff." It was Gloval's turn to interrupt. "No, you won't." He lit his briar while they all gaped at him.

Gloval said, "We've got to break through the enemy elements that stand between the SDF-1 and our home-world."

The evaluation team was aghast, Maistroff shouting, "We can't make it!"

Rick looked around and saw that everybody on his side of the table thought it was a magnificent idea. Gloval rose. "At our current speed, we are only two days from Earth, and they must have this information." He started for the hatch.

Maistroff scowled at Gloval's back. "And then what?"

The captain answered over his shoulder. "And then nothing. We just await orders while we relax, Colonel Maistroff."

He cut through all their protests. "That will be all, gentlemen."

Gloval turned to the escapees. "And as for you four..." They all shot to their feet at rigid attention.

"At least for the time being, you'll be relieved of duty. You've earned a little R and R. You're dismissed."

The four saluted him happily. "Enjoy yourselves," Gloval said gruffly; puffing his pipe. They did a precise right-face and marched out of the conference room in style. But at the last moment, Gloval removed his pipe from his mouth and called, "One moment, Lisa."

The others continued on. Lisa paused at the hatch and turned back to him. "Yes, Captain?"

"Personally, I am inclined to believe that your report is accurate. However..."

"Certainly," she said. "Thank you, Captain. I know you believe in us, and I appreciate that."

"I'm glad you understand."

The door slid open again, and she turned and left. Gloval, looking back to the debriefing team, saw that the fact that he'd chosen to tell Lisa what he did, where he did, wasn't lost on them.

"I'd rather face the aliens again than *that* bunch of brass," Max Sterling told Rick as they walked down the passageway. They were walking side by side, with Ben behind. They could hear Lisa's quick footsteps as she fell in at the rear.

"Gloval wasn't so bad, and that Major Aldershot," Ben said.

"They're only doing their job," Rick maintained. "I'd feel the same way in their place."

"Sure you would," Lisa put it, a little surprised that Rick Hunter had been so transformed from a headstrong discipline problem to a trained military man who understood why and how the service functioned. "And they'd feel exactly the same way we do in ours."

"That's right; why not look on the bright side," Ben said. Rick looked back to Ben but found himself making eye contact with Lisa. He looked ahead again quickly, in turmoil, not sure what he felt.

"After all, all of us were promoted, weren't we?" Ben went on, noticing nothing, very jolly. "And we're going home to a big hero's welcome! So why not relax and enjoy the rest and recreation Captain Gloval gave us?" He clapped Rick on the shoulder, staggering him.

Rick looked back at him sourly. "*You* could probably relax in the dentist's chair, Ben."

"Are you sure this is the right way?" Konda asked nervously, watching the elevator's floor-indicator lights count down toward One.

"We're headed for the area of greatest activity in this battle fortress," Rico said confidently. "Surely the most important concentration of military secrets will be there."

"I still think we should be trying to reach the bridge," Bron grumbled.

The elevator stopped, and the doors parted. A brilliant ray of light broke on them. The three spies stood rooted, making astounded, strangled sounds.

Before them was Macross City in all its glory. The streets were jammed with traffic; the sidewalks were crowded with busy, hurrying people. Streetlights and signs and headlights shone, as did the starlight projected by the Enhanced Video Emulation system. Display windows were filled with clothing and appliances, books, furniture, and an astonishing variety of other goods.

Rico gulped and found his voice. "There's so much to spy on! Where should we start?"

Konda drew a deep breath. "Perhaps we should just mingle with the Micronians and observe their habits."

They gathered their courage and stepped out. Humans were everywhere, alone and in pairs and bigger groups, all going every which way. Some were in military uniforms, but in general everybody was dressed differently. Reassured that he and his companions wouldn't be noticed, Bron pulled up his knee socks and smoothed the pleats in his skirt.

It took all their self-control not to shout upon seeing male and female Micronians mingling freely. No officers or overseers were in immediate evidence, although it was just as plain as could be to the Zentraedi that such hivelike activity would be totally impossible without some strong central control. Still, there were humans who strode along purposefully while others stood idly conversing and still others browsed along, glancing through the gleaming store windows.

And nobody, *nobody*, was in step with anybody else.

They started off, observing carefully. Bron said, "Well, I think there's a good chance we're going to be observing them for a very long time before we figure them out."

They came to a window-shopper, a young man staring longingly at a display in a music store, eyes fixed on a red crystal electric guitar that had three necks and a set of speakers bigger than public comcircuit booths.

"What d' you suppose he's doing?" Bron whispered.

Rico considered, then smiled in sudden realization. "Taking inventory!"

Bron and Konda murmured, "Ahh!" and nodded knowingly.

CHAPTER

FOUR

> *Due to an OVERWHELMING NUMBER OF APPLICA-TIONS, processing and mailing of membership packets for the MINMEI FAN CLUB is running several weeks behind.*
>
> *MINMEI hopes that all her LOYAL FANS will under-stand this and wants you to know that she LOVES EACH AND EVERY ONE OF YOU!!!*
>
> Macross City newspaper, magazine, and broadcast ad

THE TRIO OF MICRONIZED ZENTRAEDI CAME TO AN intersection. Before them, crosswalk signals blazed and traffic lights changed colors. The movement of vehicles and people was orchestrated somehow, but the logic be-hind it was difficult to grasp. Everything was so disor-derly, so unmilitary.

And all around them was the barrage of lighted signs and flashing neon of Macross City's "downtown." They could read the signs—at least when the logos and print styles weren't *too* fanciful—but couldn't make any sense of them. And there was so little uniformity! *Surely*, they thought, *these Micronians must be mad*.

And none of the three dared admit to the others how oddly appealing he found it all.

Rico threw his hands in the air. "What military pur-pose could all those indicators possibly serve?"

Konda glanced around at lovers strolling with arms about each other's waists, at parents leading their children by the hand, at old people enjoying coffee at an outdoor café. It was just as horrible as the intelligence reports had indicated. "You can be sure some kind of sinister force is at work here."

He started off, the other two falling in with him. "There's something strange at the root of all this, something that makes these creatures so completely unlike us. But I haven't been able to put my finger on it."

"I noticed it, too!" Rico said excitedly. "Like something's out of balance—something weird that affects all of them."

They heard laughter and shouting coming their way, and the hiss of small wheels against the sidewalk. Bron pointed. "Warriors!"

A young male and a young female sped with easy, athletic grace along the sidewalk on small wheeled contrivances barely big enough to stand on.

Their hair streamed behind them, and they whooped and laughed, tilting and swaying to steer. From their merry demeanor, the spies could see that the young Micronians enjoyed their drill and the prospect of combat.

"Gangwaaaay!" called the boy.

"Yahooooo!" sang the girl.

Trying to hide his dismay at their bloodthirsty war cries, Bron dodged, then faked the other way. The skateboarders, unaware that they were part of an interspecies skirmish, effortlessly avoided him. Bron mistook their evasive maneuvers for an attack, reversed field too quickly in the unfamiliar low-heeled pumps, and ended up on his backside.

Konda and Rico hurried to kneel at either side. "Bron, are you wounded?"

"No, Konda, but I think they suspect something."

The spies looked around apprehensively. Passersby were gazing at them curiously, sometimes murmuring to one another but not stopping or making agressive moves.

"Perhaps that was only a probing attack," Rico speculated. His voice betrayed an unusual lack of self-confidence. If the Micronians were playing such a sadistic cat-and-mouse game, they must be masters of psychological warfare.

More and more people were noticing them now, laughing outright before moving along, passing comments among themselves. Their attention seemed to be focused on Bron and his attire.

"It could be that there's something wrong with our uniforms," Rico hissed.

"I don't see any difference between our uniforms and theirs, do you?" Konda demanded as he and Rico each took one of Bron's arms and hauled the bulky warrior to his feet.

Bron pulled up his white knee socks and rearranged his string of pearls. "I don't see any difference, either. But just the same, I wish I'd chosen something a little less breezy down around my legs." He flapped the hem of his skirt in the air.

People were stopping now, staring at them, laughing and slapping each other on the arm. The female Micronians seemed inclined to look, avert their eyes, then look again, blushing and shaking with laughter.

Rico caught a few words here and there—"women's clothes," for example—and made a brief, horrified comparison study of the garments he saw all around him, and their wearers.

"That's it! It's a *female*'s uniform you're wearing!"

So, they hadn't been spotted by the Micronians' secret police. Bron had his eyes closed, almost collapsing back into Konda's arms with the mortification of it.

Konda shoved him upright. "Come on! Let's get out of here *now*!"

Nobody appeared inclined to stop them, and most were laughing too hard, anyway. They dashed off in a line, Konda leading, around a corner and down a street,

around another corner and across to a park, making sure
not to bump into anybody.

"Frat initiation," someone said sagely.

"Another bunch of drunken performance artists!" an
old man yelled, waving his cane at them vengefully.

But other than that, they drew a few puzzled glances
and nothing more. Konda had spotted an illuminated
symbol whose meaning they'd learned on their earliest
explorations, the little stick-figure Micronian near the
lighted sign, MEN.

The attendant was standing outside, whiling away the
time and watching the people go by. He watched as
Konda and Rico dashed into the men's room, not terribly
interested; he'd seen guys in a bigger hurry in his time.
Then he heard the pounding of heavy footsteps and did a
classic double take as Bron brought up the rear.

The picture of offended righteousness, the attendant
held up his hand. "Just a second, madam! Nothin' doin'!
Ladies' room to th' left!"

"Okayokayokay!" Bron veered off and ran into the
ladies' room.

There were a few relatively quiet moments, during
which the attendant looked up at the evening sky synthe-
sized by the EVE system—tonight they were recreat-
ing a northern hemisphere summer sky—and reflected
on the sorry state of the human race. Women in the
mens' room! Boy, if you weren't on your toes every
minute . . .

Distracted, wandering to the corner of the little building to look up and philosophize, he failed to notice the
dim cries of "A man!" "Get out!" and "Pervert!" that
came from the ladies' room along with shrieks and howls
of outrage.

Bron emerged from the ladies' room a moment later in
a low crawl, the shoulder of his blouse ripped, hair
askew, and face scratched in parallel furrows, several
spots on his shins promising remarkable bruises.

Panting, he took a moment to catch his breath,

slumped against a partition, preparing to move on quickly before he was attacked again.

"These . . . Micronians certainly have a warlike culture!"

Elsewhere in the park, in the Star Bowl—the open-air amphitheater where Minmei had been crowned Miss Macross—a different sort of ceremony was about to take place.

None of it fazed Max Sterling very much—few things seemed to—but Ben wasn't happy. "Hey, Max, I thought we were supposed to be resting and relaxing."

Max adjusted his large aviator-style eyeglasses, smiling his serene, mischievous smile. "Aw, what's the matter? Don't you want to be a hero? Didn't you say you were looking forward to it?"

Ben considered Max sourly. Now, here was this little guy—not even twenty yet—who wouldn't even be *flying* in one of the old-time wars. In prewar days, pilot candidates who needed corrective lenses were as sought after as those with untreatable airsickness.

And then there was Max's self-effacing style, his quiet, somehow *Zen* humility, which wouldn't have been noticeable except that he was the hottest pilot who'd ever climbed into a Veritech, and everybody knew it. Not Rick Hunter, not even Roy Fokker himself, was Max's equal, but Max just went along like a good-natured kid who was rather surprised at where fate had brought him, bashful and loyal and given to blushing. Even if he did follow the fad of dying his hair—blue, in this case.

"Aw, pipe down," Ben growled at him, but in fact Ben wasn't that unhappy. Who gets tired of being cheered? Pity them, whoever they are.

Banks of lights came up all around them, until they were standing in a lighted area brighter than brightest day. Triumphant music soared from the sound system as curtains swept aside, and the applause and cheering and whistling began, like waves hitting a shore.

Rick and Lisa, who'd been conversing haltingly and enjoying a kind of mutual attraction they couldn't seem to resist, looked relieved that the extravaganza had started. The four escapees, in full-dress uniform, stood in a line on the stage; from all around the packed Star Bowl the outpouring of joy and admiration came.

There'd been good war news and bad, and virtually everyone in the amphitheater had lost friends and relatives; besides, many in the audience were military. But *these* were four who'd gone into the very heart of the enemy stronghold and come back, and returning—*coming back home*—was something very much in the minds of the people of Macross City these days.

The master of ceremonies, a man in a loud suit with an oily voice, held the microphone right up against his capped teeth.

Rick sighed and made up his mind to put up with the show as best he could. The music was still all trumpets and drums, and the ovation was growing louder and louder. A tech somewhere turned up the gain on the mike so that the emcee could be heard.

"And here are the four young champions who have miraculously escaped the clutches of our enemy: Commander Lisa Hayes, our number one space heroine—"

Lisa was breathing quickly, eyes on the floor, Rick saw; by an iron application of will, she forced herself not to bolt from the stage; there was bravery and there was bravery, and facing a crowd took a great deal of hers.

"And Lieutenant Rick Hunter, whose flying exploits are already legendary!"

Rick *was* used to crowds, was used to taking bows and waving and soaking up the glory, from his days in his father's air circus. He could easily have played to the crowd, knew just what it was they wanted and just how to make them like him even more: the little tricks of eye contact, of perhaps singling out a child to kiss or an elderly sort to shake hands with or a good-looking woman to hug.

But he did none of that. The mission that had landed him in the Zentraedi ship and in the heart of the mad Zentraedi empire hadn't been undertaken to win cheers. Playing to the crowd was a thing that was behind him now, something out of a different life. Rick Hunter acknowledged the ovation with a bow of his head and remained more or less at attention.

He looked aside only once, to see what Lisa was doing. She was watching him.

"And here are their intrepid companions," the emcee went on in a voice so ebullient that the listeners might have thought he'd been along on the mission. "Max Sterling and Ben Dixon! To these four, we express our deepest gratitude."

The crowd did. Earth was so close now, and there was a holiday spirit in the air. A homecoming; a victory; the sight of four humans who'd gone up against the relentless enemy and come back covered with glory—these things all had the Macross City inhabitants at a fever pitch.

The emcee was holding his hands up. The uproar died a little. "There's more to come! To properly demonstrate our high regard for these young heroes, we present that singing sensation, Miss Macross herself, Lynn—Minmei!"

"Miss Macross? Minmei!" Rick had almost forgotten about the Miss Macross contest Minmei had so recently won when he'd gone out on this last mission. It felt like a century before, but it was really only a few days.

She emerged from the wings, most of the spotlights going to her—followed by an escort, a fellow in white tie and tails who carried bouquets of red roses, as if she were royalty. And she was, of a sort; the audience went wild, shouting her name and whistling, clapping.

Rick could see a cluster of people waiting in the wings—Minmei's entourage, apparently—men in expensive suits who wore sunglasses at night and stylish women with calculating looks in their eyes.

But Minmei... She was gorgeous in a frilly dress whose hem was gathered up high on one side to show off long, graceful legs. Her jet-black hair swayed behind her, and her eyes were alight. She seemed used to the spotlight, used to the devotion of the crowd. She was the same young woman who had shared so many adventures and so much privation with Rick and—at the same time —a new *persona*, a darling of the mass media.

She blew kisses to the crowd, and it went even wilder; guards at the edge of the stage, who hadn't been too hard-pressed to keep people away from the military heroes, had all they could do to keep rabid fans from getting out of control. Young girls especially were reaching out in a hopeless effort to touch Minmei, many of them crying.

"I don't know about you," Ben's voice grated. "But I'm embarrassed, being put on display like this. And just look, will you?" He held up a limp lapel that had been stiffly starched at the beginning of the evening. "My uniform's starting to wilt."

Lisa was watching Rick watching Minmei. Lisa didn't feel very much like a heroine, didn't feel strong or brave. Instead, she found herself resenting the sideshow atmosphere. What did civilians know about military achievements, anyway? Show them some beauty contest winner and they forgot all about the people who put their lives on the line to safeguard the SDF-1.

I think I'd rather be trapped back in that Zentraedi headquarters station," she blurted before she herself could quite analyze what she meant by it. Rick gave her a quick, troubled glance, then looked back at Minmei.

It was Max Sterling, calm and unflappable, who answered good-naturedly. "Well, it might never happen again, so let's just sit back and enjoy this, huh?"

Minmei held up her hands for silence, and the ovation became relative silence. She took the first of the bouquets of red roses from the man in the tuxedo and gave it to Lisa.

"Congratulations on your safe return!" Minmei's winsome smile and enthusiastic manner were difficult to resist. She had a way of putting something extra into the words, of breaking through resistance, so that whomever she was talking to virtually *had* to respond in kind.

Lisa simply couldn't think badly of Minmei—found herself saying, "Thank you very much," and meaning it, and even returning the bright smile. Minmei surprised her by shaking her hand warmly, then went on to Rick, taking another bouquet.

Lisa closed the hand into a tight fist. In those seconds Minmei had made her feel like a *friend*, as if she was all-important to Minmei. Lisa had to admit that that would be a very hard thing for anybody to resist—especially a man.

CHAPTER
FIVE

As veteran Zentraedi warriors, you will, of course, even in your micronized state, find it necessary to hide your natural superiority. Be sure to conceal your immunity to the degenerate behavioral impulses of the humans.

Breetai, from his instructions to the spies Rico, Bron, and Konda

MINMEI HAD GONE ON TO RICK, TAKING ANOTHER bouquet and presenting it to him. "And congratulations on *your* safe return, you handsome devil!"

She handed him the flowers with a wink and a laugh. He stood for a second looking as though he'd just touched a live wire. Then he blurted out, "Well! Um, thank you!"

Minmei put one slender hand to his right cheek and held him steady while she kissed his left. Fire and ice coursed through him; he remembered the moment, months before, when, trapped together in a distant compartment of the SDF-1, they'd shared a deeper, more lasting kiss.

The crowd had suddenly gone ugly. Minmei was everybody's favorite, and there was a strange current of jealousy at seeing her single out a nobody lieutenant, hero that he might be, for special treatment. She was the dream girl, the idol, the fantasy figure; an undertone of hostility ran through the crowd.

She turned to the audience without losing her merry persona. "Now, now!" she chided, shaking a finger at them in mock chastisement. Amazingly, the sounds of resentment died away as quickly as that, and people were applauding her again. To make her point, Minmei kissed Max's cheek, and Ben's, as she gave them their roses. "Congratulations ... congratulations ..."

The crowd loved it; the crowd loved *her*.

Down among the people near the stage were the three spies. At first they'd merely drifted along with the people assembling in the amphitheater, to make sure they'd eluded any Micronian pursuit. Then it had become apparent that a major gathering was taking place, and they'd set out to infiltrate it. That had proved amazingly easy.

Bron had gotten rid of his pleated skirt and knee socks and white silk blouse and even the tasteful string of pearls. He was wearing a blue turtleneck and dark slacks, although it had taken a little doing to get new clothes.

On a quiet side street, they had stumbled across a metal bin stenciled CONTRIBUTIONS FOR THE NEEDY. With some effort, the portly warrior had hauled himself into it and found Micronian male garments that fit.

The three spies concluded that keeping contributions for the needy in the difficult-to-enter metal housing served as a kind of minimum qualification test in the savage Micronian culture; any needy individual who wasn't fairly spry would be out of luck. It was a stern way to run things, the trio agreed, but no doubt very efficient.

Now, though, they looked around themselves worriedly. These Micronians were obsessed with the creature Minmei. At first the spies had thought that they'd stumbled onto a simple propaganda rally and that they'd get insights on the humans' attitudes toward the Zentraedi, but the Zentraedi had hardly been mentioned.

Instead, there was a lot of strange business with passing plants around—*flowers*, to be precise—and a very confusing level of noise and emotion, virtually all of the outpouring directed at Minmei.

Konda in particular felt that they were close to uncovering some important military secret. There was no question but that the enemy was highly motivated; perhaps some new sort of mind control technique would be revealed.

They recognized Minmei from transmissions of her that they'd intercepted on their original signal-intelligence mission, of course. She'd abandoned the bizarre armor the Micronians called a bathing suit, and wore a slightly less revealing but even flimsier cover. The trio had as yet seen no demonstration of Protoculture powers from the humans' garments, but they were still very edgy.

The crowd was still carrying on over Minmei. "Hey, what's going on? A riot?" Bron yelled over the uproar.

They were packed in together tightly by the massed crowd, but Konda got his hands onto Bron's shoulders. "Don't panic! I don't *think* it's a riot; it seems to be something else . . ."

Rico was nearly at the end of his rope, sweating and shuddering a bit; a good old fashioned anti-enemy hate rally was something anybody could understand, but this was utter chaos! He covered his ears with his hands, squeezing his eyes shut. "Oh, my head!"

He began to slump in a near faint. His companions managed to catch him somehow in the press of the crowd. Just then, Minmei came to the edge of the stage in a convergence of spotlights and the gathered residents of Macross began applauding and cheering all over again.

"Now what's the matter?" Bron asked, refering to Rico as well as the Minmei situation.

Chairs had appeared from somewhere, and Rick, Lisa, Max, and Ben were sitting uncomfortably. Minmei, angelic in the spotlights, indicated them with a sweeping gesture. "To celebrate their return, my first song this evening is dedicated to these four heroes and all the others who guard and defend us!"

She threw kisses to the crowd as the band came up, uptempo. Streamers and confetti rained down, and light effects blazed. As she threw her arms wide, she seemed to be a creature of pure light, of spirit, of magic. The streamers and confetti rained down on the crowd, too, and many joined in, joyously, knowing the words, arms around each others' shoulders.

> "Stage lights flashing,
> The feeling's smashing,
> My heart and soul belong to you
> And I'm here now, singing,
> All bells are ringing,
> My dream has finally come true!"

In a time when the most adored performers were un-approachable and inaccessible, she was somehow the exact opposite of the media sirens who reigned else-where. She was, after all, one of the citizenry, another Macross Island refugee like virtually everybody else aboard. Her success and stardom could as easily have been theirs—*was* theirs in a way.

She was one of them, and she gave herself to them totally, letting them share the moment. Her silver-bright voice soared, taking the high notes with complete confi-dence. Her slim, straight figure reflected the light back into their eyes, the joy back into their hearts.

They were a battered, war-weary community, and in a way nobody quite understood, she made them feel hope and experience a soaring elation. It had been said—and not discounted by Minmei herself—that she was a *re-*

flection of them, the military and civilian occupants of SDF-1.

Certainly there were precedents in history. Times of greatest danger and tribulation inevitably bring forth symbols.

In *human* societies . . .

The three spies couldn't quite understand it but couldn't resist it either. It had to be admitted, the gathering of humans might as easily be an assembly of Zentraedi in some ways—except that this spirit of undisguised joy was utterly weird. People swayed and laughed and forgot their problems, thinking about home, and there wasn't a single pro-war propaganda message to be seen anywhere.

Somebody threw an arm around Rico's shoulder from one side, somebody else hanging one around Bron's from the other, and they were caught up in the swaying of the throng. It so happened that the groups on either side were keeping separate time, one going one way while the other went counter.

"This must be some kind of tribal ceremony," Konda speculated, but he found himself enjoying it.

Still, somehow, as easily as if they'd been doing it all their lives, the Zentraedi sorted out the conflicts and in a moment were swaying along with the thousands upon thousands of others. It began to dawn on them what they were seeing.

As had happened before, a symbol had arisen, and Minmei was it, uniquely suited to the role. One tiny Micronian female, hoping to get home, possessed of a kind of deathless optimism; and all that was set off by remarkable singing skills and a personality that won over whomever she encountered. And none of it was calculated; people sensed that. She was wonderful and straightforward, and Macross City threw itself at her feet.

She's incredibly dangerous to the Zentraedi cause, Rico mused. *Why do I like her so much?*

"I feel incredibly primitive," Bron reported dubiously.

"But it has a pleasing effect on the senses," Rico was honest enough to admit.

"It's—*mass hypnosis!*" Bron burst out, even though he'd been trained to recognize mass hypnosis and knew this wasn't it.

"Yeah, but I kinda like it," Konda confessed. They swayed along with the music and laughed at the people who swayed and laughed with them . . .

> "Stage fright, go 'way—
> This is my big day,
> This is my time to be a star!
> And the thrill that I feel
> Is really unreal:
> I can't believe I've come this far . . ."

In the midst of the performance, people had forgotten about the four forlorn figures sitting on their chairs, very much in the background now but unable to make an escape. Only Max Sterling seemed unbothered and happy.

Rick shifted the bouquet on his lap despondently. He saw it all now: Minmei had been elevated to a different level of existence. What they had gone through together and felt for each other didn't matter anymore. He had lost her.

Lisa leaned toward him to ask, "What's the matter, Rick?"

He shook himself, drawing a deep breath. "Nothing. The light bothers my eyes, is all."

Lisa saw it wasn't true. She hadn't gotten to be a commander and the SDF-1's First Officer by being unobservant or slow to understand what was going on. But that didn't help her figure out what she was feeling as she looked at Rick and the now-unreachable Minmei: some complicated mixture of relief and foreboding.

Minmei's hands were high, and she had moved the crowd into a veritable transport of joy. White light blazed all around her, and it seemed that every hope and aspiration was embodied in her.

> "I can't believe I've come this far,
> This is my time to be a star!"

The hatch to the battle fortress's bridge slid aside; all heads turned. Gasps and yells sounded from all sides.

Lisa felt better already, there in the place that was most important to her. "Hi," she said shyly, not recognizing many of the faces and wishing only to get back to her station, get back to her work. She would have died before admitting that she wanted to drive all other thoughts out of her mind—to forget.

Claudia placed one hand to her chest in a "mercy me" sort of pose. "The prodigal returns!" The dark face creased in lines of real welcome, and Lisa began to feel better.

Gloval was absent from the bridge. The relief-watch tech at Lisa's usual station stepped away from it, glad to see Lisa but a little intimidated before the omnipotent superwoman. "Nice to see you again," the enlisted rating squeaked.

Lisa, nervous as a cat, managed to meet her eye for a moment. "Thank you very much," Lisa got out, essaying a smile and then hiding behind her thick curtian of brown hair again. "It's nice to be back."

She ran her fingertips across the console's controls, lost in thought. There had been so many times when she'd never expected to stand there again.

The women on the bridge were paying her a kind of attention that didn't really conform to any conventional military courtesy—happy for her and taking liberties with standard procedure.

"Congratulations on your promotion!"

"And you're a real hero!"

"We're all so proud of you, Lisa!" The tech who'd

been watching over Lisa's station had her hands clasped, smiling beatifically.

These were all women who had served their time under fire, who had come to know what it was Lisa Hayes did so well and how much of a difference her actions had made in the fate of SDF-1. Their few words meant so much more to her than the spotlights and crowds—she felt her tension ease; she was home again.

Now that she was back in familiar surroundings, everything that had happened came back to her. A small part of her was preoccupied, sifting through her emotions, but Lisa just savored the contentment of being back where she belonged.

The things that had brought conflict to her—the kiss in the enemy stronghold, the sight of Rick and Minmei— were, perhaps, aberrations. Maybe it was just her destiny to be what those in her family had always been—members of a military dynasty, her destiny tied to that of the SDF-1.

Certainly, all things seemed clear there on the battle fortress's bridge. Doubts, misgivings—they fell away like dead flower petals.

Then Claudia was leaning an elbow on the console, too good a friend not to understand exactly how Lisa felt, too good a friend not to kid her out of it. "Well, how does it feel to be a heroine?" she purred.

Lisa's pale cheeks colored. "Oh, you!"

"Come on! Tell Aunt Claudia!" The dark eyes narrowed mischievously. "Or did this promotion give you a sudden sense of modesty?"

Lisa lowered her gaze to the deck, avoiding eye contact as she often did when she wasn't on duty. But she grinned at Claudia's jibe, the first time she'd grinned in a while. She gave her friend a bemused smile.

"That's it! My secret's compromised!" Lisa crossed her arms on her chest and made a severe face, imitating Captain Gloval at his sternest. She rolled her r's, so there'd be no mistake. "So let's have a little *respect* here!"

Somebody Lisa didn't recognize returned from a coffee run, and they all had some. "It's good to be here," Lisa said meditatively, letting the cup warm her palms. Then she made a puckish expression. "And lemme tell ya, the Zentraedi make lousy coffee."

Claudia realized something and set her cup down. "Hold on! Lisa, I thought you were supposed to be on special furlough."

Lisa lowered her cup, not wanting to think too hard about the ceremonies and the tangled feelings that had driven her back to the bridge. She bit her lower lip for a moment and said, "I wanted to come home."

Claudia was about to say something to that; Lisa was both shielding something and waiting for someone to draw her out about it. It seemed to Claudia Grant a good time to order the enlisted crew off the bridge for chow or whatever and get down to business.

But just then the hatch slid back again, and the Terrible Trio stood there. Sammie, Kim, and Vanessa spied Lisa and charged in, the dignity of rank forgotten. Lisa forgot it, too, swapping hugs with them and loving the calm and strength and serenity of the SDF-1's armored bridge.

Claudia filed the subject of Lisa's furlough and her strange new introspection away for discussion in the near future. She'd been protective of Lisa ever since they'd met and tried not to let that spill over into nosiness, but—

This girl needs a talking to, Claudia decided. *And I'm not even sure about what!*

CHAPTER
SIX

As an insect seen through an enlarging imager may appear a monster, so these Micronians, magnified by a few minor successes and by an unforgivable timidity among certain Zentraedi leaders, are permitted to resist us. This has led to a stalemate; what Zentraedi worthy of the name would permit this?

Khyron the Backstabber

THE JEEP ROARED DOWN THE EMPTY SDF-1 PASSAGE-way, rounding corners on two wheels, tires shrieking. Ben Dixon enjoyed this kind of outing; he usually took a slightly longer route to the fighter bays than he had to because he so missed the open road.

Ben's dragster had been parked in an alley on Macross Island on the day of the fatal spacefold maneuver. So now it was either a floating relic in space back near Pluto's orbit or had been completely dismantled by the salvage and reclamation people. Either way, he didn't like to think about it.

But barreling around the roomier parts of the dimensional fortress helped ease his loss. The civilians had crowded-but-very-livable Macross City, but once in a while *some* people needed to hit the road, floor the accelerator, and let off a little steam. It was an open secret that some of the less traveled regions of the SDF-1 had become virtual racetracks.

Ben took a corner even more sharply than usual and waited for Rick, who was sitting in the seat next to him, to make a perfunctory objection. But, lost in thought, the Vermilion Team leader didn't say anything. Sprawled in the back, Max Sterling looked supremely unworried. Ben was a little bit offended by that; Max was a good friend, but Ben expected passengers to be a little *intimidated* when he drove. Yet nothing seemed to ruffle Max or dim the boyish cheerfulness for which he'd become famous.

In fact, a few guys had decided that Max's good-naturedness meant that he was a wimp despite his ferocious flying skills. There'd been a few fights, and Max had insisted that Rick keep Ben from interfering on his friend's behalf.

Help wasn't necessary, anyway; Max's astonishing reflexes and hand-eye coordination more than sufficed. Max always helped his opponents to their feet afterward, still with that boyish smile; he even performed first aid in one extreme case. After a while, interest in bothering Max Sterling waned.

Max gave his blue hair a toss and resettled his glasses, turning at the sound of another jeep engine. He leaned forward to tap Rick and point; at the wheel, Roy Fokker was catching up to them, accompanied by three of his Skull Team fliers.

"Hey, Rick!"

"Hi, Roy."

"Uh oh." Roy came up *very* close alongside, and Ben had to cut the wheel to avoid an accident.

"Where d' you three think you're going?" Roy demanded.

They were on one of the longest straightaways in the ship, but they were moving fast. Ben knew he was being tested; he sweated a bit but kept on a steady course. But they were approaching the far bulkhead at an alarmingly rapid speed, and there was room for only one jeep in its hatchway.

The Skulls in Roy's jeep didn't seemed very thrilled about the encounter either, but they knew better than to say anything to their hotheaded leader.

"What'd you say?" Rick asked mildly.

Roy hollered, "I said, where d' you think you're going?"

Max leaned forward. "The PA system said for all military personnel to report for duty!" he said. Ben Dixon began sweating bullets as the far bulkhead got closer and closer.

"You had orders to stay behind, you nitwit! That announcement doesn't apply to you guys!" Roy was shaking his fists in the air; the guy riding shotgun grabbed the wheel while one of the others in the back seat began crossing himself and the other spun a tiny prayer wheel. Roy ignored them, keeping the accelerator floored.

"But that wasn't an order...specifically," Rick pointed out.

Roy had his hands back on the wheel. "Well, I'm *making* it an order! Specifically! Return to quarters, and make it fast!"

Ben eased back, breathing a sigh of relief. Roy's jeep took the lead as Rick yelled, "Gonna take on the enemy alone, huh?"

Roy turned and rose, his front seat passenger diving for the wheel again. Roy shook his fists at the heroic escapees. "Maybe you'd rather report to the brig for insubordination?"

Ben began braking. He and his friends chanted in perfect unison, "Not really, sir! No thank you, sir!" a bootcamp response used here to mock Roy by implying that he was as dumb as a drill sergeant.

Roy cracked an unwilling smile, then turned to take the wheel back from his ashen-faced front seat passenger. "I'm glad you understand," he called back, voice growing fainter. "Nobody likes a smart aleck!"

Ben stopped just short of the bulkhead, and Roy's jeep shot through the hatch, speeding toward the fighter bays.

"There goes a wonderful guy," Ben said, letting out his breath.

The Zentraedi had a saying that in Earthly terms would translate to: "Even wolves may be prey to the tiger."

So the huge armada kept its distance from SDF-1, pacing it on its homing journey. Ironclad orders stated clearly that Zor's fortress was to be captured with all its Protoculture secrets intact. From the perspective of the fleet's commanders, the more important point at the moment was that the SDF-1's main gun had proved itself operational, even though the Micronians had used it very sparingly.

The Zentraedi couldn't figure out why—one of the mysteries that prompted the placement of Bron, Rico, and Konda aboard SDF-1. What the Zentraedi *didn't* know was how little the human race understood about the giant ship and how vulnerable the SDF-1 really was.

All the Zentraedi knew for certain was that the ship contained enough power to destroy whole star systems and rip the very fabric of space and time. So the armada paced the battle fortress, watching and waiting.

A report was being delivered by a technician in a fleet command vessel. "Commander Azonia, the super dimensional fortress had started to increase its velocity."

Azonia looked up sharply at her intelligence analyst. Azonia sat in the control seat amid a vast array of machinery and consoles and holographic data displays that stretched away in every direction.

"What are your orders?" the analyst asked. Azonia glanced at the various maps, readouts, and tactical projections.

"Dolza has given me no authority to destroy it," the armada's commander replied, running a hand through her close-cropped blue-black hair. "So we'll just follow it and see what happens." Azonia had replaced the legendary Breetai as commander when he'd made one mistake too many, and she had no intention of suffering similar humiliation.

The analyst bowed obediently, and withdrew from the command center. Azonia pulled her campaign cloak tighter around her and adjusted the high collar; she was having doubts she would never betray to a subordinate.

The Micronians' homeworld was close; what would happen there? The original Zentraedi invasion force had smashed all Terran opposition until it encountered those thrice-damned Robotech mecha—the Veritechs. And after all these months, who knew what *new* defenses the perversely ingenious humans might have developed?

Allowing the super dimensional fortress to reach its destination was a risky game at best; a disastrous one, perhaps. Yet Azonia couldn't see any new orders coming from her superiors, nor could she come up with an alternative course of action to offer them that didn't risk the loss of the all-important secrets of Protoculture.

Azonia forced down those thoughts. There was still time to win, and victory in *this* campaign would bring the most precious prize in all the universe.

The SDF-1 was in its cruiser mode, which meant that the great main gun couldn't be fired. This was unavoidable, however, since the giant weapon would function only in Attack mode—a formation that rendered Macross City virtually uninhabitable.

In its present configuration it looked like a conventional spacecraft or even a naval vessel. The Thor-class suppercarriers *Daedalus* and *Promethus* were swung back flush against it, and the two great booms of the main gun were mated together to form a prow. The bridge and its attendant structures rose above the main deck but still sat rather low.

As its gargantuan thrusters flared blue fire, the ultimate warcraft approached the orbit of pockmarked Luna.

Claudia studied Earth's moon in her displays. "We are proceeding at maximum speed, Captain," she reported. "Beginning Earth-approach maneuver... *now*!"

Gloval appeared to be asleep: The polished visor of his cap was pulled low down on the bridge of his nose, and his arms were folded across his chest. But he said quite clearly, "Vanessa, how has the enemy fleet reacted?"

Vanessa pushed her glasses up, made a final sweep of her instruments to be sure, and then turned to Gloval. "They're still all around us, Captain, but they're maintaining distance. It's strange—they're still matching our speed exactly."

Gloval rubbed his cheek and realized he needed a shave. He didn't even want to *think* about how tired he was. "It would appear they still don't want to risk firing on the SDF-1. This would seem to bear out your theory, Lisa."

Lisa broke her intense concentration on her instruments to say, "I certainly hope so, sir." If she was wrong, the battle fortress wouldn't last another hour.

"We are approaching the orbit of Luna, Captain," Vanessa said tensely.

"Keep monitoring the enemy closely."

"Yes, sir."

Lisa chimed in, "Fighter ops reports Vermilion and Ghost teams ready for takeoff, Captain." She did her best to sound businesslike and not think about one of those Vermilion Team Veritechs. Especially its pilot...

Gloval nodded and hoped he wouldn't be forced to use them. They were some of his very best pilots, but they'd been chewed up badly in the latest installment of the running battle the SDF-1 had been fighting for months in the remote, dark places of the solar system.

Earth was so close. Gloval would have given his own

life without an instant's hesitation if it would have meant repatriating all the refugees who'd survived the brutal voyage. But that wasn't how things worked.

In a Zentraedi command center, a finger the size of a log stabbed at a tactical display screen representation of the SDF-1 and the armada around it.

Khyron could barely keep his voice from breaking in rage. "The Micronian ship is *here*, and the ships under my command are *here*, behind it. Now, at maximum speed, their vessel stands a good chance of penetrating the net around it and escaping!"

He stared angrily at his second in command, Grel, and his trusted subordinate, Gerao. "Are we to sit here with our arms folded while these creatures get away and not raise a finger to stop it?"

"But Azonia has forbidden us to act," Grel pointed out. "What can we do?"

Khyron slammed his palms down on the display console. "We will crush them!"

Khyron, handsome and fiendish commander of the Zentraedi Seventh Fleet and its mecha strike arm, the Botoru Battalion, had a reputation that gave even the giant warriors pause. He had *earned* the nickname "Backstabber": He had a reputation for savage ferocity, a total lack of feeling for his own men, and an unquenchable thirst for bloodshed and triumph.

Grel knew better than to contradict his superior when the killing rage was upon him. There was a persistent rumor that Khyron's secret vice was the essence of the Flower of Life, a forbidden addiction; if that were so, he used it in some form that made it a flower of death. In this mood, he was capable of anything.

"Order the lead ships in the squadron to increase speed and attack!" he roared, holding his hand high in a salute and gesture of command. "For the glory of the Zentraedi . . . and of *Khyron!*"

* * *

Vanessa stared intently at her screens, calling out, "A squadron of enemy battle cruisers has broken away from the rest of the fleet and is moving in on us, Captain. Approximately ten of them."

Gloval stared out the forward viewport morosely. "Scramble fighters."

"Yes, sir." Lisa drew a deep breath, opening the PA mike. "Vermilion and Ghost Teams, scramble, *scramble*!

Down in the hangar decks of the supercarrier *Daedalus*, there was the controlled chaos of a "hot" scramble, one that everybody knew was no drill. The huge elevators began raising the Veritechs to the flight deck port and starboard, two to a lift.

Roy Fokker pulled on his flight helmet and checked his controls as his ship was moved out for lift by a tow driver. Roy was Skull Leader, but experienced pilots were in such terribly short supply and Rick and the others were on enforced R&R, so he had to help fill the ranks of the depleted Vermilions, especially at a critical time like this.

The Veritechs' stabilizers and wings began sliding into flight position. Cat crews rushed to hook up and launch the fighters; The Veritechs went into a vigilant holding pattern, ready to fend off any attack against the VTs that were still vulnerable, awaiting launch.

The cats slung the fighters out into space; the blue Robotech drives flared, and the Vermilions and Ghosts formed up to do battle yet again.

Gloval had hoped to avoid it, but he gave the order nevertheless. "Engage SDF-1 transformation and activate pin-point defensive barrier. We are breaking through the alien fleet!"

"Macross City evacuation is nearly complete, Captain," Sammie told him.

The voices of the others kept up a constant, quiet

flow of orders and report. "All sectors begin transformation." "All section chiefs please report to the bridge."
"Damage crews stand by." "Emergency medical and rescue personnel ready, Captain."

Banks of screens showed interior and exterior scenes,
the frantic haste to brace for attack and reconfiguration.

Once again the awesome, incredible, and perilous Robotech transformation of SDF-1 was about to take place.

It had been hard to get used to the bustle and activity
of Macross City, but this sudden abandonment of it was
even stranger.

The three Zentraedi spies still had no idea what was
happening. The PA announcements were bewildering,
impossible to understand. The trio was hesitant to show
ignorance at first, but by the time they'd worked up the
nerve to start asking questions, everybody was scurrying
in a different direction and answers were impossible to
get.

Now they found themselves standing at the center of
a deserted intersection as traffic lights and crosswalk
signals blinked through their accustomed sequences. The
EVE system was shut down, the artificial sky gone,
leaving only cold, distant metal high overhead.

"Everyone's vanished," Rico said slowly, pivoting
through a 360-degree turn. It felt very spooky to be
standing in the middle of an empty city.

"What d' you think that announcement was?" Konda
asked. "What could it be—this 'transformation' they're
talking about?"

Bron was about to add something when the street
began to quake beneath them, tossing them around like
water droplets on a griddle. As deep grinding noises
began, they were thrown to the surface, so they tried to
cling to the pavement. They could feel the vibrations
through the ground.

Then the street parted beneath them and an enormous
sawtooth opening widened rapidly. Despite his hysterical
scrambling, Rico disappeared into it.

What they never asked themselves was whether Khyron would have behaved as he did if it hadn't been for the accursed Micronians! I hated Micronians, too; we all did. It was just that Khyron was better at it.

Grel, aide to Khyron

REACTING FASTER THAN BRON, KONDA JUST MANaged to grab Rico's sleeve and keep him from falling beyond reach. Then Bron was there to help pull his companion back out of the abyss.

It was a long drop, into a type of machinery they hadn't seen in the battle fortress before. Rico lay puffing and gasping, white-faced. "What kind of insane place *is* this?"

Elsewhere, the titanic booms that were the battle fortress's bow were rotated to either side by monster camlike devices. Whole sections of hull moved and slid, opening the ship's interior to the vacuum of space as precious atmosphere escaped. Giant armor curtains slid into place to seal the gaps, but not before there was grievous loss of the very breath of life. The SDF-1's life support systems would eventually replace it, but the inhabitants of Macross would be living under the same atmospheric conditions as Andean Indians for a while—if they survived.

Enormous pylons the dimensions of a city block rose from the floor and descended from the ceiling, crushing the buildings in their way. The grinding of servomotors shook every bolt and rivet in the ship.

Scraps of buildings, torn loose by the outpouring of air, were whirled around like leaves in a cyclone. Macross City was being leveled.

The three spies went dashing down the middle of a broad, empty street, dodging a falling sign here, a broken cornice there. Utility poles toppled, whipping live power lines around like snapping, spitting snakes. Konda puffed, "I think it would be advisable for us to take cover as soon as—"

He never got to finish. Just then, the ship's internal gravity fields shifted from the effect of the massive power drains of the transformation.

The three went floating into the air among drifting automobiles, scraps of roofing material, uprooted trees, and spinning trash barrels.

All through the great fortress, modules shifted, and billboard-size hatches closed here, opened there.

The full-ship transformation had the two Thor-class flattops, *Daedalus* and *Prometheus*, swinging out from the SDF-1's sides by the elbowlike housings that joined them to the ship. The midships structure that housed the bridge and so many other critical areas rotated, coming end for end into the center like a spinning torso.

Inside, cyclopean power columns met and latched as cables snaked out to connect with them and complete the new configuration.

Gloval fought to stifle his impatience; the ship was nearly helpless while undergoing transformation, but there was absolutely no way of hurrying it. And there was no alternative: The SDF-1's main gun *couldn't* be fired in any other configuration because the ship space-fold apparatus had simply vanished after that first disastrous jump from Earth to Pluto. The transformation was a kind of glorified hot-wiring, bringing together components that would otherwise be out of each other's reach.

"Starboard wing section transformation seventy-five percent complete," Vanessa said.

"Port wing section transformation complete," Kim added. "Now connecting to defensive power system."

"Enemy vessels approaching in attack formation," Lisa said, her face lit by her screens. "Estimated intercept in fifty-three seconds. Ghost and Vermilion teams on station to engage."

The battle fortress had become a tremendous armored ultratech warrior standing, straddle-legged, in space, awaiting its enemies. They swooped at it eagerly.

"The enemy's within range of our main gun, sir," Kim said.

From Vanessa: "Fighter ops reports all Veritechs clear of the line of fire."

"Transformation complete, Captain," Sammie told Gloval.

"Fire!" Gloval growled.

The safety shield had been retracted from the main gun's trigger. Lisa pressed the red button hard.

Tongues of starflame began shooting back and forth between the booms that constituted the gargantuan main gun, whirling and crackling like living serpents of energy.

The blizzard of energy grew thicker, more intense. Then it leapt away, straight out from the booms, merging and growing brighter until suddenly there was a virtual river of orange-white annihilation, as broad and high as the ship itself.

The hell-beam tore through space. The first ten heavyweight warships from Khyron's contingent flared briefly, like matches in the middle of a Veritech's after-blast. In a split second their shields failed, their armor vaporized, and they were gone.

Khyron's handsome face was distorted like a maniac's. "We must press the attack! Move the next wave in!" The Zentraedi warrior's code could forgive audacity —even direct disobedience—from an officer who *won*. But defeat might very well be unforgivable and earn him the death penalty.

More heavy ships-of-the-line moved up, firing plasma cannon and annihilation discs. The SDF-1 shook and resounded from the first hits. There were a few gasps on the bridge, but Gloval and the bridge crew concentrated on their jobs.

The enemy dreadnoughts' blue-fire cannon volleys rained on the SDF-1 as Khyron's second attack wave bored in.

The three green-white discs of the dimensional fortress's pin-point barrier system, each bigger than a baseball infield, slid along the ship's surface like spotlight circles. The disaster of the spacefold equipment's disappearance had left the vessel unable to protect itself completely; the pin-point system was the stopgap defense developed by the resident Robotech genius, Dr. Lang.

Now, the female enlisted-rating techs who operated the pinpoints sweated and flickered their eyes from ship's schematics to threat-display screens to readouts from the prioritization computers. In a frantic effort to block enemy beams they spun and twirled the spherical controls that moved the pin-point barrier shield loci across the ship's hull.

The circles of light slid and flashed across the battle fortress's superalloy skin. Enemy beams that hit them simply dissipated, changing the locicircles into a series of concentric, rippling rings for a split second. Then the circles came back to full strength, racing off to intercept another shot.

No one had ever done that kind for work before, and

the three young women were good at what they did—experts by necessity. But sometimes, unavoidably, they missed . . .

The SDF-1 shuddered at another impact. "Starboard engine has been hit," Claudia informed Gloval without looking up from her console.

Gloval said nothing but worried much. Even now, a decade and more after the SDF-1's original appearance and crash landing on Earth, nobody understood very much about its enigmatic, sealed power plants—not even the brilliant Lang. What would happen if an engine were broached? Gloval didn't spare time to worry about it.

The bad news was coming fast. "Industrial section hit." "Sector twenty-seven completely nonfunctioning."

Claudia looked to Gloval. "The pin-point barrier is losing power."

Gloval didn't permit himself to show his dismay. *Now what?* he thought. *We've fought so hard, endured so much, come so close.* "Keep firing the main battery!" he said, aloud.

Lisa knew how to read him so well after all these years. *Look at him*, she thought. *It's hopeless! I know it!*

"Lisa, didn't you hear the order?" Claudia was yelling, a little desperately.

"Yes," Lisa said resolutely. She pressed the trigger again.

Another unimaginable flood of utter destruction leapt out to devour the second Zentraedi wave.

In her command center, Azonia watched a dozen proud Zentraedi warships vanish from the tactical display screens.

"That imbecile Khyron! What does he think he's doing? He has no authority whatsoever for this attack!"

Yaita, her aide, said laconically, "No, Commander." Then, "Therefore, what are your orders?"

In an event of this magnitude there was opportunity for the right junior officer to get herself noticed, perhaps even mentioned in dispatches to Dolza's headquarters. Interfering with the unstable battle lord risked a confrontation, perhaps even combat, but by nature Yaita was a risk taker.

Azonia, even more so. "I shall have to force Khyron to break off his attack myself."

Yaita said, "You mean to divert part of the fleet blockade? But the enemy vessel might find a way to break through!"

"It can't be avoided," Azonia said coldly. "That ship must not be destroyed. Its Protoculture secrets are the key to the Zentraedi's ultimate victory."

Vanessa relayed the information, "The aliens are bringing up reinforcements, Captain; nearly two hundred heavy warships." She looked up from her console. "Analysis indicates that's too many for us to handle."

"The barrier's weakening rapidly," Sammie said.

"We're losing power," Kim added.

Vanessa watched her tactical screens, ready to give the grim details as the enemy closed in for the kill. But she suddenly had trouble believing what she was seeing. "What's going on? The reinforcements are breaking formation—spreading out and closing in on the other enemy ships!"

Khyron watched his trans-vid displays furiously as Azonia's fleet swept in to close with his own reduced forces. "What is that woman up to now?"

The Micronian vessel was nearly his; he could feel it. *I will not be thwarted again!*

A projecbeam created an image of Azonia in midair over his head. "Khyron, you *fool*! Dolza has given you no authority whatsoever to destroy the Earth ship!"

Khyron felt that insane wrath welling up in him once

again, a fury so boundless that his vision began to blur.
He growled like an animal through locked teeth.

Azonia was saying, "As commander of this force, I
am ordering you to cease this attack at once and with-
draw to your assigned position—or you will find *yourself* facing Zentraedi guns!"

Studying the tactical readouts, Grel said, "Captain,
her entire arsenal is already being aimed at us."

Khyron crashed his first on the map console. "That
blasted meddling idiot of a woman!"

He may have been called Khyron the Backstabber by
some, but he'd never been called Khyron the Suicide or
Khyron the Fool. Azonia had the rest of the armada to
back her in this confrontation.

Khyron had no choice. With Azonia's ships blocking
their way, his vessels reduced speed, and the SDF-1
began to put distance between itself and its enemies.

"They're escaping!" Khyron's voice was a harsh
croak. "And so Azonia robs me of my triumph. But I
swear: I shall not forget this!"

Grel had heard that tone in his commander's voice
before. He smiled humorlessly.

If Azonia was wise, she would begin guarding her
back at all times.

The immense Robotech knight that was the SDF-1
descended to Earth's atmosphere, toward the swirling
white clouds and the blue ocean.

"I don't understand it," Claudia said. "They screened
us from their own attack."

"I know, but we'll worry about that after we get back
to Earth, Claudia," Gloval answered.

"Reentry in ten seconds," she told him.

"Steady as she goes, Lisa," Gloval ordered calmly.
All the equations and theories about how the recon-
figured SDF-1 would take its first grounding in Earth-
normal gravity were just that: theories. Any one of an

almost infinite number of things might go wrong, but there was no alternative. Soon the ship's crew and inhabitants would find out the truth.

"Atmospheric contact," Claudia reported.

The giant warrior ship descended on long pillars of blue-white fire that gushed from its thruster legs and from the thrusters built into the bows of *Daedalus* and *Prometheus*. "Order all hands to secure for landing," Gloval directed.

Elsewhere, the strain was beginning to tell. Power surges and outages, overloads and explosions, were lighting up warning indicators all over the bridge.

"Starboard engines have suffered major damage from the reentry, sir," Claudia said. "And gravity control's becoming erratic."

"The explosions have caused some hull breaches, Captain, and we're losing power quickly," Lisa put in.

"This is going to be some splashdown," Gloval muttered to himself. At least the loss of atmosphere didn't matter anymore; in moments they'd either have all the sweet atmosphere of Earth to breathe or they wouldn't need air ever again.

Claudia counted off the last few yards of descent. Vast clouds of steam rose from the ocean as the waters boiled from the heat of the drive thrusters. Then the ship hit the water.

At first, the ocean parted around it, bubbling and vaporizing. Then it came rushing back in again, overwhelming even that tremendous heat and blast. SDF-1 sank, sank, the waves crashing against its armor, then racing away from it, until at last it disappeared from sight beneath the churning water.

Moments passed, and the sea began to calm itself again. Suddenly, a spear of metal broke the surface; then three more: the long tines at the tips of the booms of the ship's main gun. The booms rose, shedding water, and then the bridge. The SDF-1's shoulder structures came up, and then the elbow housings, until at last *Daedalus* and *Prometheus* were up, their flight decks shedding millions of gallons of water.

The calculations were right; SDF-1 was an immense machine, but it was quite buoyant and seaworthy. It gleamed brightly as the seawater streamed down its hull.

CHAPTER EIGHT

> *"There's no excuse for sloppy discipline—not even victory," Colonel Maistroff was fond of lecturing us. Maybe so, but I never saw a haircut win a battle.*

The Collected Journals of Admiral Rick Hunter

GLOVAL AND HIS BRIDGE CREW GAZED OUT AT THE serene ocean. The Terrible Trio was intoxicated with joy.

"Home again—after so *long!*"

"It's just beautiful!"

"Home—"

Sammie, Vanessa, and Kim, arms around one another, turned to the others. *"Welcome back!"*

Claudia was brushing tears away, and Lisa just stared at the sea, not knowing exactly what she felt.

Gloval lit his pipe; regulations be hanged. "Now, how about a little fresh air?"

Major access hatches began cranking open all around the Macross City area; light and wonderful sea breezes flooded in. Blinking and gaping, the inhabitants of the city began to congregate in the air locks and on the outer decks.

When they finally believed what their senses were telling them, the cheering began—the backslapping and hugging and kissing and laughter. People stood in the sunlight and cried or prayed, shook hands solemnly or jumped up and down, sank to their knees or just stood, staring.

Kim's voice came over the PA. "We've touched down in the Pacific Ocean. The captain and crew extend their gratitude to the citizens of Macross for your splendid cooperation during a difficult and dangerous voyage. It's good to be home."

A big hatch dropped open just below the bridge. Ben Dixon was the first one out onto the open deck, laughing and turning somersaults, leaping into the air ecstatically.

More Veritech pilots and crew people rushed after him. Rick and Max stood watching Ben carrying on. "He'd make a pretty good acrobat, wouldn't he?" Max commented.

Rick smiled. "Probably, but—look at that blue sky. That's no EVE projection! I can't say I blame Ben a bit."

Ben was pointing into the sky. "Look! They're giving us a fighter fly-by to welcome us!"

So it seemed; twenty or more ships that resembled VTs, bearing the familiar delta markings of Earth's Robotech Defense Forces, came zooming in in tight formation to pass over the SDF-1.

But the three pilots felt their joy ebb as they were struck by the same thought: The Zentraedi were still out there, millions of ships strong.

An endless series of details kept Gloval busy for the next few hours, including the recovery of the Vermilion and Ghost fighters who'd flown escort during the SDF-1's final bolt to safety.

But at last he put aside other duties, satisfied that subordinates could take care of the remaining details, and repaired to his cabin to complete his compilation of log excerpts.

The Earth authorities would soon have all the facts as he knew them. Gloval wondered if the leaders of the United Earth Government would believe all that had happened to the SDF-1 in the months since it had disappeared. Sometimes Gloval himself had trouble.

He reviewed the long tape he'd compiled to amplify the other materials. Starting with the initial Zentraedi attack, when so much of Earth's military force had been obliterated and the dimensional fortress had activated itself, the log covered all the important incidents of the running battle with the aliens.

There'd been the ghastly aftermath of the spacefold jump and the almost insurmountable problems of getting tens of thousands of Macross refugees settled in the ship. The *Daedalus* Maneuver, Lisa Hayes's inspiration, had allowed the humans to win their first resounding victory amid the icy rings of Saturn.

Lisa saved the day again, this time on Mars, by destroying the alien gravity mines that had been holding SDF-1 on the Red Planet's surface. The ship's most recent crisis began when radar was disabled by enemy fire, leading to a foray by a Cat's-Eye recon ship—piloted by Lisa Hayes, of course.

Gloval didn't like to think too hard about the fate his command would have suffered if he hadn't been lucky enough to have had Lisa with him. Certainly there were skilled and courageous men and woman throughout the SDF-1; examples of extreme bravery and ingenuity were too many to mention. But it seemed that Lisa's devotion, valor, and special loyalty to the SDF-1 and to Gloval made her the pivotal figure in almost every action the ship fought. It made it that much more difficult for Gloval to see how few real friends Lisa had, how empty her life was of anything but service and duty. Of course, he had no right to interfere with her personal life, but he couldn't help being worried about her.

The most important thing Gloval had to present to the United Earth Government was an enigma: The molecular and genetic structure of the Zentraedi was so formidable that some of them could even survive unprotected in the vacuum of space for short periods of time; their sheer physical strength was a match for that of Battloids and other human Robotech mecha—yet they had nearly collapsed at the sight of two relatively tiny humans sharing a kiss.

Moreover, the Zentraedi didn't seem to know anything about *repairing* their equipment. It was as though they were a servant race using the machinery given them by some higher power, yet they boasted of being the mightiest warriors in the known universe.

Gloval shook his head, hoping the Earth authorities would have additional information or analyses that would shed some light on the mysteries surrounding the war.

He worked for hours, inserting updates and clarifying things that warranted it, condensing wherever he could. Twice he dozed briefly, then got back to work, making an occasional status-check call to the bridge. The relief officer on duty, Lieutenant Claudia Grant, assured him all was well.

A quarantine area had been established around the battle fortress—not surprising, Gloval supposed—and a communication blackout had been imposed for the time being. The crewpeople took that fairly well—they were used to military discipline—and even the civilians had been too delirious with joy to be very upset by it so far. Gloval could see why his superiors might want to maintain radio silence until he'd appeared to give his full report, but he hoped the need for it wouldn't last much longer.

The civilians were still celebrating, but they wouldn't be satisfied with that indefinitely.

He brought the tape to a close, puffing on his briar as he dictated. "I am convinced the Zentraedi have more firepower than we can even imagine. The situation is extremely critical, and I believe that a central issue in this war they've forced on us is this mysterious 'Protoculture' they keep mentioning. I therefore suggest that— what? Come in!"

The rapping had been gentle. Lisa entered with a pot of fresh coffee. "I thought you could use some about now, sir."

"Thank you; it smells wonderful." She came in, and the coffee's aroma filled the cabin, cutting the aroma of the pipe tobacco.

She poured while he glanced up at an ancient brass ship's clock on his wall. "I did not realize what time it was."

He put the pipe aside. The ashtray lay next to a detailed analysis and history of living arrangements and social organization in Macross City and the SDF-1 during the voyage. The SDF-1 held far and away the largest human population ever to travel in space, and that on a voyage of very long duration. The data on how people had coped with their living conditions and somehow managed to make things work would be very important, Gloval suspected. There would have to be a lot more humans in space for long periods of time, sooner than anyone expected.

Gloval threw back the curtains, looking out the high, wide curve of viewport at a Pacific dawn. He'd forgotten how many seemingly impossible colors there could be in such a sunrise—the purples and reds and pinks. He'd forgotten how the water broke the light into a million pieces and the sky ignited.

"Here you are, sir," Lisa said, handing him his cup, prepared just the way he liked it. They gazed out at the peace and powerful beauty of the dawn.

"I never thought I'd see anything as beautiful as this ever again," Lisa said. It was a moment of such tranquillity, such oneness with the planet that had been their goal for so long, such satisfaction with a protracted, seem-

ingly hopeless mission accomplished at last, that she did
her best to lock it in her heart and senses and memory—
a treasure that she could relive occasionally. Sparingly.

"You're right," Gloval said at length. "I feel the same
way. You know, I have a confession to make."

Lisa sipped her coffee, watching the sea, saying nothing. Gloval went on. "I had a premonition when I took
command of this ship, the feeling that something terrible
would happen. It's difficult to explain, but it was a con-
viction that something would happen to us that would
change us forever."

She studied his face. "And it seems that you were
right."

He was staring at the sea and the rising sun, though
she doubted he was really seeing them. "This ship still
has its secrets, Lisa, but *what are they*? We must find
out; I can't escape the feeling that *everything* depends on
it."

It was strange to see the flight deck crews working in
conventional coveralls and safety helmets again after
months in vacuum suits, strange to think that most
planes would *need* a catapult launch from the SDF-1 and
the flatdecks now in order to get up airspeed.

Theoretically, the transport that was waiting for Gloval and Lisa didn't need a launch; it was a VTOL job,
capable of lifting off like a helo. Still, it had the reinforced nose and landing gear of a naval aircraft, and SOP
recommended that fixed-wing aircraft receive cat launch.

Gloval walked toward it with Lisa at his side, his atta-
ché case weighted with documents, tapes, photographs,
reports, and evaluation reports on *those* reports. His feet
scuffed against areas of missing nonskid surface on the
flight deck, flaps of it having been peeled loose by the
violence of SDF-1's homecoming.

Scores of crewmen were just completing an FOD
walkdown of the flight deck, pacing its length in a line
abreast running from port to starboard. Foreign Object

Damage was a thing much to be feared on a carrier; no scrap of debris could be left to be sucked into a jetcraft's air intake.

The weather remained fair, but now a thick odor rose from the sea. The superheated steam and hard radiation produced by the dimensional fortress's touchdown had resulted in a considerable fish kill, even so far out at sea; the sun was warming the foul-smelling soup that lapped around the hulls of the carriers and the approximate hip level of the SDF-1's "torso." Still, the stench came from far below and was easy to endure, mixed as it was with the trade winds that carried Earth's inimitable air to people who had been breathing reprocessed gases for months now.

Gloval was tight-lipped and silent, feeling strange premonitions like the one he'd mentioned to Lisa. The United Earth Government's replies to his messages had been terse, noncommittal. It seemed he had another desperate job of convincing to do.

Lisa emulated her captain, saying nothing and betraying nothing by her expression as she followed him up the boarding ladder into the transport. A crew member closed the hatch, and the transport's turbines increased their howl.

The plane had already been boxed—aligned on the catapult and fitted with an appropriate breakaway holdback link that was color-coded for its particular job. The transport's downswept wings bobbed minutely as the catapult crew got ready to launch.

When the cat crew had gone through their ritual, the transport shot away, taking lift from the sudden flare at the bow, off the angled flight deck, in a cloud of catapult steam.

Kim stretched, arms behind her head, gazing down at the carrier deck from the SDF-1's bridge. She sighed. "Well, there they go; at least they got a clean launch."

She was standing at the vast sweep of the bridge's

forward viewport with Sammie, Vanessa, and Claudia, following the transport's climb.

Little Sammie shook her long, straight locks of blond hair back from her face. "I wish I were going, too," she said forlornly, resting her chin on the viewport ledge.

Claudia unwillingly told herself that it was time to scold a little, not sympathize; these last few hours or days before the SDF-1 crew was relieved might be the most demanding of all where discipline was concerned.

So she chided, "What're you talking about, Sammie? D' you know how *cold* Alaska is this time of year? Or any time of year? You should be glad you're staying where it's warm."

"Well, I'm not," Sammie said bravely.

"At least we'd be off the ship," Vanessa pointed out, adjusting her glasses self-consciously. She and Kim nodded supportively and made low "uh huh!" sounds.

Claudia was suddenly stern. "All right, that's enough of that! First off, the captain and Lisa are on a classified mission, which means we don't talk about it any more than we have to for duty purposes. And we *don't* mention it at all outside this bridge, *do you roger that transmission?*"

The Terrible Trio nodded quickly, gulping, in unison.

The hatch slid aside as a voice startled them. "*Good* morning, ladies! I'd like—"

The greeting was cut off by a sharp *whap*! of impact. The bridge crew turned in surprise, Sammie letting out a small cry. Claudia maintained her composure, but it wasn't easy.

"Oh! Ouch! Uhhhh!" Colonel Maistroff was in the hatchway, rubbing his forehead, his cap knocked back cockeyed on his head by the impact, holding himself up with one hand against the frame.

Everyone there knew Maistroff, and not for any cordial reason; one didn't make allies of the bridge crew by crossing Captain Gloval.

Claudia fluttered her eyelashes and said disingenuously, "Colonel, are you all right? That hatchway's *terribly* low! I recommend you duck down when coming onto the bridge, sir. Captain Gloval always does."

There was something in the expressions of the bridge crew that said that they resented Maistroff's taking this liberty; it was his right to act as if he were Gloval, but they were not required to play along with the pretense.

Maistroff rubbed a growing knot over one eye, making a low grating sound so that subordinates wouldn't hear him groan in pain. "Thank you for that warning, Lieutenant Grant; you're only about ten seconds too late."

He stopped rubbing his forehead and squared his cap's visor away. The Terrible Trio trooped past him, in step, on their way to their duty stations. "I just came up to officially take over command of this vessel in Captain Gloval's absence."

Claudia held all her personal feelings in check; she'd had a taste of what command was now and was willing to give even Maistroff the benefit of the doubt. "Yes, sir; I'd heard that you would. I'm sure you'll enjoy the experience."

He glowered at her. "Mmm. I don't think that 'enjoy' is quite the appropriate word, miss. But I do expect to run a tight ship." He moved past her, going to the forward viewport.

Claudia tried to get a grip on herself. *Tight ship!* She'd had the feeling he'd say that. *As though Captain Gloval runs a loose ship! As if Captain Gloval isn't the best skipper in—*

"No more slipping around the rules," Maistroff was saying. "What this bridge needs is a good dose of discipline." Gazing grandly out the forward viewport, he drew a long cigar from the breast pocket of his uniform jacket.

It was plain that he was savoring the moment. Perhaps he had saved the stogie all this time since the SDF-1's accidental departure so that he could smoke it on the bridge as master. Maistroff made a production of biting off the end, rolling the cigar between his fingers, and moistening it front and back between his lips.

His indescribable pleasure in the moment was broken by a high-pitched voice. *"There's no smoking on the bridge, sir!"*

"What?" Maistroff whirled on Sammie, who was out of her chair and didn't look in the least daunted by his scowl.

"It's on page two of the ship's SOP rule book—standard operating procedure, isn't it, sir?"

Claudia couldn't for the life of her figure out whether Sammie was serious or was having her little snipe at the colonel. Apparently, neither could Maistroff.

He turned back to the viewport, holding the cigar as if somebody else had put it in his fingers, not willing to throw it away but unable to do much of anything else with it. His back was ramrod straight, and his cheeks flushed a bright red.

"Ah, of course. I was only holding it. I had no intention of lighting it." He gritted his teeth but refused to take official recognition when he heard female giggling and tittering behind him.

"Excuse me, Colonel," Claudia said. "Will there be anything else, sir?"

He turned to her, trying to put down his anger, cold cigar clenched in his teeth, hands clasped behind him. "What? What?"

She said gently, "I was officer on the last watch, sir. Am I relieved?" She saluted.

He was doubly red-faced to have forgotten so simple a thing as relieving her of the command. "Oh!" He answered her salute. "Sure, you go right along, Lieutenant Grant. I'm sure we'll be able to operate just fine until you get back." He smiled indulgently.

As Claudia gathered her things, Maistroff went to inspect the rest of the bridge and incidentally try Gloval's chair to see how it felt. Making sure that he wouldn't hear, Vanessa whispered to Claudia, "Y' better check in later to make sure the bridge is still *here!*"

The Terrible Trio stifled their laughter. Claudia smiled. "You hang in there, girls."

Reflecting that Maistroff didn't know what *real* opposition was like but would find out if he crossed the Terribles, Claudia left the bridge.

CHAPTER
NINE

Hey, I was managin' a couple of other class acts when I signed Minmei, y' know? I mean, I wasn't just chopped liver, kapish? I mean, I had the Acnes, who had a big, fat bullet: "I'll Be a Goo-goo for You."

Anyway, Minmei-doll hits the scene, and I can't even get my other acts arrested! "Minmei! Minmei!" People don't wanna hear anything else.

The public—go figure.

Vance Hasslewood, Minmei's personal manager, interviewed on Jan Morris's on-ship TV show, "Good Morning, SDF!"

THE CITY OF MACROSS HADN'T SEEN FIREWORKS since that fateful day when the Zentraedi first appeared in the solar system. There had been plenty of explosions, all right, but not simple skyrockets and colored bursts.

Now, fireworks flashed high over *Prometheus*'s flight deck. Canopies and marquees were set up, and an old-fashioned town festival was in progress.

Strings of firecrackers banged and snapped on the nonskid, and streamers and confetti flew in squalls, carried by the sea breezes. Many had chosen to wear costumes, and some wore fantastic, gruesome giant masks that covered them from head to foot. There was dancing and laughter, a sort of communal drunkenness with joy.

On an improvised speaker's platform, Mayor Tommy Luan held his hands high. "Our troubles are finally over! Let's make this party last all week!"

The stocky little mayor's good friend, Vern Havers, a lean, mournful-looking man with a receding hairline, clung to the side of the platform to call up anxiously, "But what about packing? Shouldn't we be getting ready to *leave*?"

"Vern, this isn't a day for packing! We have plenty of time for that! Don't you think that the Macross survivors deserve a celebration after all we've been through?"

The mayor looked up at the looming SDF-1, its silent guns throwing long shadows across the deck. "Besides, once we leave this ship, we'll probably never see it again."

Vern hadn't even thought about that, but it made sense; SDF-1 would have to take up its job of guarding Earth; the rebuilt Macross City would of course be dismantled.

Like many others, Vern had dreamed of returning to Earth, had lived for it, all these months; but now, like many others, he felt strangely sad that a unique time in his life was ending. He hoped there could be some kind of open house or something so people could see what the citizens of Macross had accomplished before all their handiwork was swept away.

"Well," he said, "if you put it that way, I suppose you may be right."

The mayor was literally hopping up and down, from his own swelling emotions. "Of *course* I'm right! Now, let's party!"

Vern resigned himself to the inevitable. It *was* good to be back on Earth, but he was beginning to realize how difficult it would be to get used to uneventful peacetime life.

Elsewhere in the milling, boisterous crowd, the three Zentraedi spies were trying to absorb what they were seeing around them.

Gaiety like this was unknown among their people; certainly the frivolous consumption of food and drink, scandalous mingling of males and females, and pointless merrymaking would be a court-martial offense among the warrior race.

Konda was absorbing something else—his third cup of an intriguing purple liquid with ice cubes floating in it—when Bron, gawking at all the goings-on, jostled his elbow.

Konda, vexed when some of his drink spilled, gave the bigger spy a shove. "Clumsy! Can't you be more careful?"

Bron looked hurt. Konda said, "I'm sampling something called 'punch,' and you interrupted my experimentation."

Bron looked at the beverage dubiously. "It seems to me you've imbibed more than is necessary for a mere effects test, Konda."

Konda pushed the cup into Bron's hands. "Here! You try it! I know where to get more, and the requisitioning procedure is puzzlingly informal." He hiccuped.

Bron sniffed the stuff suspiciously; then, after a final glance at Konda to make sure he showed no sign of toxic reaction, he downed the punch in two big swallows. It was cold but somehow had a warming effect. He gagged a little but felt a pleasant sensation course through him.

"I don't know what's in this stuff," Konda said with a foolish grin, "but it sure is getting *me* charged up!"

Oh my goodness! thought Bron. "You . . . you mean it's got some kind of Protoculture in it?"

Exasperated, Konda was considering clouting Bron in the head for being such a dummy, when Rico rushed up to them angrily. "Why aren't you two making noise like the rest of these people? You want them to notice us? Well then, pretend you're having fun!"

Rico, too, held a cup of the punch; it was all but empty, and he looked a little bleary-eyed. He threw one fist up and yelled, "Yay-yyy!" so loudly that he quite startled his companions. "We finally made it back! We're home again!"

"Hurrah! We beat the enemy!" Konda added helpfully. "Hurrah for us! Hurrah for Earth!"

"Down with the Zentraedi!" Bron burst out, doing a little jigging dance step. That punch beverage, whatever it was, had him feeling rather, well, *happy.* "Up with the Micronians! Down . . ."

He realized the other two were staring at him. Bron covered his mouth with his hand in anguish. "Oh, my! I didn't know what I was saying! Konda, Rico—please don't report me!"

Just then a young woman dressed as a medieval princess and carrying two cups of punch swept by. She saw the three standing together, one without a cup. She put her extra one into Konda's hand and clinked glasses with them, grinning behind her silvery domino mask. "To home and friendship!" Then she was gone in the crowd.

The three spies looked at one another for a moment, then echoed, "To home and friendship," and clinked cups as the celebration swirled around them.

With most of the off-duty crew and virtually all the civilians up at the party, SDF-1's passageways were empty, giving the ship a haunted feel. Making her way toward the VT pilots' living quarters section, Claudia Grant tried to put that fool Maistroff out of her mind and concentrate on enjoying her brief time off watch.

For the first time in months, the Veritech pilots weren't flying constant patrols or combat missions, and SDF-1 was being manned by a virtual skeleton crew. So her free time meshed with Roy's for the first time in a long time.

The love affair between Claudia Grant and Lieutenant Commander Roy Fokker, as passionate as it was romantic, had been terribly strained by the demands of the SDF-1's desperate voyage. But now there would be time to be together—the very best thing about the dimensional fortress's return, as far as Claudia was concerned. She signaled at the hatch to his quarters but got no response. Rapping on it with her knuckles was no more effective.

Claudia wasn't about to miss her chance to see him. Perhaps he'd left her a note. She tapped the hatch release and entered as the hatch slid aside.

Roy Fokker—leader of the Veritech Skull Team, heroic ace of the Robotech War—lay snoring softly, dead to the world, his long blond hair fanned out on the pillow. At six foot six, he hadn't yet found a military-issue bunk that fit him; his feet and the covers stuck off the end of the bed.

It had been said of Roy that "he doesn't *fly* a jet; he *wears* it." But right now Roy looked like nothing so much as a sleepy kid.

For months we never have the chance to be alone, and when the opportunity finally arrives, he sleeps through it! But she couldn't be mad at him. He'd been on duty, usually in the cockpit of a fighter, just about every waking hour since the spacefold jump.

Poor dear; he must be exhausted. "Oh, well . . ." She pulled the covers up over his shoulders, then turned to go.

"Hey, hold up!" She turned to see Roy sitting up in bed, blinking the sleep away, smiling. "You just gonna run off?"

She grinned at him. "I figured the Skull Leader needs all the beauty sleep he can get."

"You were wrong. C'mere."

He grabbed her wrists, his big hands engulfing hers, and pulled. Claudia gave a laughing yelp as he dragged her down next to him, then relaxed against him in a kiss that took away all the pain and sorrow and weariness of the long voyage home.

Back in the midst of the festivities on *Prometheus*'s flight deck, Rick Hunter stood waiting next to an aircraft. He was wearing his old flying circus outfit of orange and white trimmed with black, and his silken scarf.

The plane was the fanliner sport ship won by Lynn-Minmei when she'd taken the Miss Macross title. This was to be its maiden voyage in the atmosphere of Earth.

It was a sleek, beautiful propfan design by the illustrious Ikkii Takemi himself, with powerful, pinwheel-like propellers in a big cowling behind the cockpit. It reminded Rick very much of his own *Mockingbird*, which depressed him because that in turn reminded him of the time he'd spent with Minmei, stranded together in a remote part of the SDF-1. During that time she'd come to mean so much to him, but now...

"You're a lucky guy, Rick, to be flying Minmei home," a ground crewman was saying. "You not only get to leave the ship, but you spend time with a beautiful—huh?"

Rick heard it, too, and looked around. The roar of the crowd had increased, and there was cheering and applause.

"Like I said," the ground crewman went on, "you get to spend time with a beautiful celebrity."

Minmei's entrance was worthy of her star status—her *superstar* status, as far as the crew and passengers of the SDF-1 were concerned. She was being chauffeured across the flight deck in a glittering new Macross City–manufactured limo, the crowd parting before her. They held up signs with hearts and fond sentiments on them or waved autograph books somewhat hopelessly.

Flower petals and confetti and streamers rained down on her car; people pressed up against the glass to smile, wave, and call out her name—to feel close to her, if only for a moment.

"Y' know, she's the only one who's been given permission to leave the ship so far, even for a short time," the crewman continued. "Hope you enjoy the ride."

Minmei sat quietly in the exact middle of the limo's rear seat, hands folded in her lap, watching the people throng around her car and pay homage. She wore her old school uniform: white blouse and necktie, brown plaid blazer, plaid skirt. Audience research indicated that her public liked to see her in attire that emphasized her youth.

Her manager, Vance Hasslewood, sat next to the chauffeur, happily surveying the crowd. "Well, this is quite a turnout for you, Minmei."

Minmei gave a little sigh. "Yes, I suppose these mobs are the price one must pay for fame."

Hasslewood and the uniformed chauffeur exchanged a wry, secret look.

"Could we go a little faster? I'm late as it is," Minmei added. The driver sped up a bit, honking his horn, and Minmei's adoring public had to move out of the way quickly.

I wonder if she's changed much, Rick thought as the limo screeched up beside the little sport plane. Minmei had promised that she and Rick could still see a lot of each other once he joined the Robotech Defense Forces, but between his duties and her skyrocketing career as the SDF-1's homegrown media idol, that promise had been forgotten.

The chauffeur held the rear door open for Minmei while Vance Hasslewood went to confer with a liaison officer from the SDF-1 Air Group.

"Hello, Minmei." Rick smiled. "It looked like you had a lot of trouble getting through that crowd back there."

She giggled, her eyes shining in the way he remembered. "Those are my loyal fans. They follow me everywhere. I just *love* them!"

She turned to wave to the people being held back by a cordon of security guards. "Hello, hello! Thank you for coming down to see me off! I love you all very much!"

Apparently she was unaware that a lot of the people, the majority of them perhaps, were simply there for the party; maybe she didn't even realize that there *was* a celebration going on. Rick shook his head, laughing; Minmei was sweet and charming, but she still lived very much in a world of her own.

The fans were clapping, stamping, and whistling for her, waving their signs and banners. Vance Hasslewood looked on approvingly, eyes hidden behind tinted glasses.

"Thank you!" she called, throwing kisses.

"Boy, they really like you," Rick remarked.

"I know," she said matter-of-factly. "Rick, when can we take off? I'm really anxious to see my parents."

"Well, I guess we can take off any time; the engines are all warmed up."

He led her to the boarding ladder. "Just climb into the rear seat—careful, now—and sit down, strap yourself in."

She got into the fanliner and settled her shoulder purse next to her, taking up the safety harness. "Thanks, Rick. It seems like you've become a lot nicer now than when we first met."

Huh? Minmei *was* still living in her own world, he saw—revising her memories of the past according to her preferences, forgetting whatever was inconvenient or troubling or replacing it with something that freed her from introspection.

So now she'd decided that Rick had been unkind to her. Perhaps she'd forgotten that he'd saved her life several times . . . forgotten that they'd held a mock wedding ceremony and she'd worn the very white silk scarf that he now had around his neck as a bridal veil.

Perhaps she'd forgotten their kiss, there in the remotest part of the ship. Certainly she was now surrounded by people who would go along with almost anything she said or chose to think, people not eager to remind her of her past life and ties. She was free to be completely self-absorbed.

As he stood on the boarding ladder looking down into the cockpit at her, he saw her in a new light. "Maybe I've grown up, Minmei."

Her brows met, and she was about to ask what he meant; but just then Vance Hasslewood, standing at the foot of the boarding ladder, thrust his face up into Rick's. "Young man! Your name; what is it, hah?

Rick threw him a sarcastic salute. "Lieutenant Rick Hunter, sir."

"Well, Lieutenant Rick Hunter, I expect you to take good care of Minmei! She's a very busy person, and she must get back to the ship on time."

Minmei surprised both men by jumping in on Rick's side. "Don't worry, Vance! I feel perfectly safe! Rick's a *very* good pilot!"

Hasslewood backed off a bit. "Er, yes, I'm sure he is, but he's so *young*, I, uh—"

Rick wondered just who and what Hasslewood really was. Certainly, Minmei's astounding popularity had been very lucrative for the man, and he was very proprietary about her. But what else was there to the manager-client relationship?

Nothing romantic, Rick was pretty sure of that; even at her most career-hungry, Minmei wouldn't have fallen for an abrasive hustler like Hasslewood. But *how* had Minmei gotten permission for even a brief visit to her parents when the SDF-1 was virtually quarantined?

To be sure, Rick's confidential orders were specific enough: Make sure that Minmei had no access to outside media interviews. Just the family visit, and then right back to the SDF-1, *whatever that took*.

Rick had thought about Minmei's brief liberty privilege and could only come up with one explanation: Her talents and appeal had been a major factor in keeping up morale and fighting spirit during the long return voyage to Earth. And no matter what the public information people were saying, the war wasn't over and there was still a threat of invasion. If Minmei could do for the general population of Earth what she'd done for the people on SDF-1, she would be a tremendously important resource. That gave her and, in turn, Hasslewood, an awful lot of leverage.

Right now, though, Rick wasn't worrying about influence or power. He stuck his face into Hasslewood's, cutting him off. "How about standing back? We're taking off now."

Hasslewood just about fell over his own feet, retreating. "Sure, kid; don't get touchy! Have a good trip, Minmei! Hurry back!"

Rick pulled on his goggles and headset, lowering the cockpit's front and rear canopies.

Vance Hasslewood mopped his forehead with his handkerchief, watching as Rick increased the propfan RPMs. The manager prayed silently for a quick, uneventful flight; all his personal marbles were riding in that rear seat.

Rick turned the fanliner's nose and taxied. The sport plane wasn't equipped for cat launch, but it was so little and light that there was more than enough runway for a takeoff. With *Daedalus*'s bow turned into the wind, the little ship fairly leapt up off the deck.

Minmei sighed happily, looking down at the SDF-1, savoring the freedom of the flight. "Ahhh! It's been a long time!"

"It sure has," Rick murmured, bringing the plane onto its course for Japan. A vivid, seductive fantasy had begun running in the back of his mind, of being forced to land with Minmei—marooned on some idyllic desert island, perhaps; of things being the way they once were.

"I forgot how I felt about her."

"What?" Minmei asked, leaning forward to peer around his seat.

He hadn't meant to say it aloud. Flustered, he hastened, "Oh, nothing, nothing!" But his face was reddening, and she looked at him oddly.

He tried to concentrate on his flying as she settled back in her seat. But that little fantasy just wouldn't let him alone.

CHAPTER
TEN

We weren't deaf to the innuendo, of course. Claudia and the Terrible Trio and I heard all the sniping about "Gloval's Harem," though people were very careful not to say anything around Claudia after she decked a cat crewman.

There is a loneliness to command, it's no myth. But there's also an area around the commander—where you're not in charge but not part of the rest of the ship's complement, either—that's often a difficult place to be, too.

Lisa Hayes, *Recollections*

THE UNITED EARTH GOVERNMENT'S COMMAND complex was like a landlocked iceberg—only a fraction of it was visible aboveground. In fact, the communications towers, observation and surveillance structures, defensive emplacements, landing pads, and aircraft-handling facilities constituted less than half a percent of the cubic area of the enormous base.

It was still a highly classified installation. The fighters escorting the transport plane bearing Gloval and Lisa wouldn't have hesitated for a moment to open fire on any unauthorized aircraft that entered its restricted airspace and failed to respond to their challenges.

Changing the angle of its engine blast, the transport eased in for a vertical landing. Lisa, glancing out her viewport, saw Battloids pacing on guard duty.

Once the plane's authenticity and clearance were verified, its landing pad became an elevator, lowering it deep beneath the bleak, subarctic landscape.

Lisa and Gloval released their seat belts and gathered their things.

"I hope they're prepared to listen," Lisa said. "Captain, we've *got* to convince them! Surely they'll listen to reason!"

"That would be nice for a change," Gloval growled.

The Ikkii Takemi—designed fanliner rolled and soared, glinting in the sun.

"Woo-hoo-ooo!" Rick exulted. Piloting a Veritech through deepspace had its appeal, but there was nothing like feeling control surfaces bite the air and making a light stunt plane do exactly what you wanted it to.

"Having fun, Minmei?" He laughed again, and she joined in. He adored the sound of her laugh.

Maybe, he thought, he could just set down on some little island and say he wanted to check out the engine. Then he'd have a chance to talk to her, would have her full attention for a while.

While he was turning the idea over in his mind, a familiar voice came over his headset. "Veritech patrol to Minmei Special. Hey, Lieutenant! It's Ben and Max!"

"Huh?" Rick saw them now, back at five o'clock. The fighters had their variable-sweep wings extended all the way for the extremely low speed needed to keep pace with the sport plane. He was a little embarrassed that they'd managed to sneak up on him.

"We understand you have a VIP aboard," Ben went on.

"Some guys have all the luck," Max added suggestively.

"We're returning to base; have a nice date," Ben finished, laughing. The Veritechs waggled their wings in salute, then peeled off onto a new course. Their wings swept back to an extreme angle as they picked up speed, punching through the sound barrier.

They were doing better than Mach 2 and still accelerating when Rick lost sight of them. "So long, wise guys," he called over their tac net. "See you later."

"Ben and Max are silly, but it *does* sort of feel like a date."

He felt his pulse race. "Yep."

She inhaled the cold, clear air, watching the glitter of the sun on the canopy. "It's great to get away for a while, but when I get back, I have a whole lot of work to make up. You should *see* all the things they want me to do!"

Show biz again! "I suppose it fills your time," Rick snapped, vexed.

She hadn't noticed his tone, ticking off her projects on her fingers. "Oh, yes! I've got to do a television show, and then I'm cast in a play. Why, I'm even supposed to do a movie!"

"Mmm," Rick tried to sound elaborately bored. She still didn't notice.

"That's going to be really great," Minmei gushed. "I expect to work really hard. This *is* my first movie, y' know. Say! If I speak to the director, I might be able to get you a small part, hmm?"

That made him smile. Maybe she did think about others after all, notwithstanding the fact that he thought movies were a rather brainless occupation and definitely inferior to flying a fighter.

"Maybe some other time, Minmei. But, hey, where d' you get all your energy? Flying heel-and-toe patrols is one thing, but I'd be exhausted trying to keep up with a schedule like that one. Minmei?"

He hiked himself around to look over his seat at her. "Minmei, are you all right? Speak to me!"

For a moment he was afraid the cockpit had lost pressure and looked to his instruments frantically. Then he saw what had happened. "Well how d'you like that? She's asleep."

Her chin was resting on her chest, and she was breathing softly. Again, Rick felt a wave of that fierce protectiveness he'd felt toward her when they were stranded. And tremendous affection rose up in him as well.

He turned back to his piloting with a fond smirk. *I hope she wakes up long enough to say hello to her parents.*

The streamlined tramcar, mounted on twin magnetic-lift rails, plunged deeper and deeper into the gigantic headquarters installation.

Aboard, Captain Gloval sat with arms folded across his chest and cap visor pulled down over his eyes, as if asleep. He would have loved a meditative pipe but knew how unpleasant that would have been for Lisa.

Lisa shifted nervously on the padded passenger bench. "Will it take long to reach the Council chambers?"

Gloval lifted his visor. "Just a little longer. The shaft goes down almost six miles." He didn't remark on his disdain for all this burrowing and hiding—Earth's governing body skulking at the bottom of a hole in the ground like frightened rabbits! When the Zentraedi were capable of blowing an entire planet to *particles*!

"By the way, that reminds me," he went on. "Have you heard anything about this Grand Cannon?"

Lisa's face clouded; the words sounded so ominous. "No, what is it?"

"It is a huge Robotech weapon that's been under construction here for almost a decade now."

Gloval gestured to the illuminated schematic of the base that was displayed by the tramcar's access doors. The elaborate details of the sprawling underground complex were mostly represented in coded symbols for security's sake; but the essential layout was in the shape of a gargantuan Y. The blinking light representing the tramcar was moving down one arm of the Y, heading for the vertical shaft.

"The Grand Cannon uses Earth's gravitational field as

its main energy source," he told her. "In fact, the shaft we're traveling in at this moment is the barrel of the weapon."

Lisa looked around uncomfortably. "You mean, if this base were attacked right now and Command decided to fire the cannon, we'd be blown away?"

Gloval chortled. "Well, I'd like to think they'd clear the barrel first."

He knew she was astute enough to see the major disadvantage of the great gun: Even with the Y arrangement and the titanic rotating gear, the Grand Cannon's field of fire was very limited—and even United Earth Command hadn't come up with a way to tilt and traverse the planet Earth to bring the weapon to bear on inconvenient targets. Arrangements to overcome the problem were part of the plan, of course, but . . .

Gloval had been one of the loudest voices against the project; wars, he maintained (with history on his side), aren't won by defense but rather by offense—by an SDF-1 that could go out and confront the enemy, not by a Grand Cannon in a hole in the ground.

He had gone head to head with Lisa's own father during that argument, taking the opposite side from a man who had been a valued friend and a comrade in arms until then. It had been the beginning of a rift that had only widened and deepened in the years since.

It made him sad to reflect on those days gone by— they had saved each others' lives . . . they were bonded by more than mere blood. Yet Admiral Hayes had become an opponent, almost an enemy.

Henry Gloval knew the way of the world and of highest-echelon politics; he was as shrewd as anyone who played the game. But there was still something in him, something bred in the bone, that found it bewildering and saddening that there could be such a falling out between men who'd served together in war.

I suppose it's just as they say, he thought. *I'm a peasant at heart, and there's no changing that.*

He shook off his brief distraction. There was an Isaac Singer story he'd taken to heart—"The Spinoza of Market Street"? Perhaps; in any case, the point was that the virtue lay in *behaving* in accordance with one's ideal, not necessarily in *being* it.

And one of Henry Gloval's ideals was a steadfastness in friendship. So he asked Lisa pleasantly, "Your father never brought you down here before?"

"A few times," Lisa answered, "but I was never allowed to come down the main shaft. Now I understand why."

"Yes, this Robotech project was top secret. Only a few outside officers had access. It made the old-time Los Alamos reservation look like open house!" He chuckled; there were fond memories of those days among the bitter.

"And no civilian visitors," he finished, "not even an admiral's daughter."

Lisa wore a puzzled look. "But then, why did they let Father in?"

Gloval said staunchly, "Who else was there? He was the visionary. He pushed for the creation of this complex when no one else thought it was necessary."

She looked around again, looked to the vast schematic on the wall. "My father was responsible for all this? I didn't know that!"

Gloval drew a deep breath. "Your father was always decisive." How could he talk to her of friction and resentment? He couldn't.

"When I was serving under him in the Global Civil War, a problem came up about inadequate rations for the troops. When Admiral Hayes didn't get satisfactory action from headquarters, he led our entire Combined Action Group in a raid on the logistical depot. Camo face paint; real *guerrilla* stuff!

"He personally sat on the log-command three-star general while we got something to eat. There were a lot

of brave and deserving men and women who had their
first real meal in a long time that night."

Lisa was laughing heartily, one hand at the base of her
throat. "My father got away with *that*?"

Gloval was laughing again. "It's true. The general
thought sappers had infiltrated the base, kept sending
down orders for us to find them. There wasn't a woman
or a man in that entire unit who wouldn't have done
anything, *anything*, for your father, Lisa. Would've followed him to hell if he'd given us the word."

Lisa was still laughing, shoulders shaking. But her
laughter no longer had anything to do with the story
about her father. The sudden freedom from the SDF-1,
the astonishing size of headquarters base, the very emphatic and yet somehow empty joy of being home again
had cast a certain familiar pall over her. It was strangely
overwhelming; there was nothing she could do but laugh.

Lisa Hayes had realized a long time before that a life
in the military didn't exactly make for happily-ever-after,
particularly for a woman. Nevertheless, there was a
warmth of that moment, something between people
who'd served together, something no outsider could
have ever shared.

"It's good to hear you laugh again, Commander."
Gloval smiled slowly. "I think this is the first time I have
heard you laugh since you escaped from the enemy, no?"

Lisa said, "Ahh," and "Umm," trying not to think of a
particular VT pilot, trying to keep the warmth and the
laughter alive, doing her best not to be vulnerable to de-
sires and attractions and yet be open to Gloval's confes-
sions. A small part of her wondered if male subordinates
of *female* flag-rank officers went through this.

"But I wonder if we'll feel much like laughing after
this meeting with the governing council," Gloval went
on. "It's crucial that they be made to understand that the
aliens are *only* interested in the battle fortress and its
secrets, *not* in our world."

Gloval tilted his cap forward on his brow again. "I hope you've thoroughly prepared your arguments, Commander Hayes."

Her chin came up; her eyes shone. "Ready to go, Captain," Lisa said, managing a smile as she was reminded of the loneliness she felt.

All her life, it had been so difficult for her to establish a relationship with men her own age, even men in the military. But it was not surprising, really; she had been surrounded by men like Gloval, men like her father. How many men like that could there possibly be? One in a hundred thousand? In a million?

Hard to match, in any case.

Gloval was saying, "Mm-hmm, that's good."

Lisa replied, "I'm sure we'll be able to convince them. After all, *we're* the only ones who've had close contact with the aliens!"

Yes, Gloval reflected, it would seem so cut and dried to her; Lisa's father was one of the most powerful people on Earth, but despite that—perhaps *because* of that— Lisa herself was completely naive about political machinations.

He knocked a bit of ash out of the bowl of his pipe and tamped down some new tobacco, as was his habit when he was thinking. Just as he struck one of the old-fashioned kitchen matches he so loved, a surveillance eye in the wall lit up and a feminine computer voice said, "ATTENTION! SMOKING IN THIS CAPSULE IS FORBIDDEN! PLEASE EXTINGUISH ALL SMOKING MATERIALS IMMEDIATELY!"

Gloval yanked his briar from his mouth guiltily. "Ah? Can't I smoke *anywhere*? If it's not my bridge crew warning me, it's these machines!"

Lisa was clearing her throat meaningfully. "Captain, are you worried about the SDF-1? Sir, *is something going to happen to us*?"

Gloval's aching conscience made him leap on the question, "Why do you ask?"

Lisa only smiled and said, "When something's bothering you, I've noticed, you always pull out your pipe and make a big production about lighting it."

Gloval lowered the pipe slowly and, not caring who might be listening on some bugging device, said, "Hmmph! I must confess I'm very worried about this meeting. I'm not sure these—" he made a gesture with his head to indicate his disdain for anyone who would protect themselves underground while ordering brave men and women to die "—not sure these men will listen to us with open minds. And Lisa, *it's vital to our future that they do so, do you understand*?" Gloval spread his broad, brown peasant's hands on his knees and looked down at them.

Lisa nodded slowly. She was Admiral Hayes's daughter, used to having people view her as an access road to the highest levels of decision; *that* was one of the things that set Lisa Hayes so far apart from her contemporaries.

She'd seen power politics *in excelsis* all her life, had sickened of them and the unspeakable people drawn to them.

After Karl Riber had died she felt she would never heal from that hurt. But surely there were others out there, people who were kind and patient and true? The image of Rick Hunter suddenly came to her. Though she refused to admit it to herself, Rick Hunter had come to mean very much to her.

"What will happen if we can't convince the Council?" she asked Gloval.

He answered in a grim, level voice. "Then the Earth will go to war against the aliens."

Before, he had always spoken of triumph and the need to win; this time, with only Lisa to hear his confession, Gloval mentioned nothing about that. Lisa knew

him well enough to know what that meant: Captain Gloval's estimation of the human race's chances against the
Zentraedi were very bleak indeed.

The tramcar came to the bottom of the Y's arm and
began the vertical descent to the innermost chambers of
the United Earth Defense Council.

CHAPTER
ELEVEN

Did You Ever See a Dream Walking?

Early twentieth-century song title

"MINMEI? MINMEI, WAKE UP; YOU'RE AL-
most home."

She stirred a little; it was a voice she liked, she knew,
and it was a message that was wonderful beyond com-
pare. Minmei yawned charmingly against the back of one
hand, trying to stretch but restrained by something. Her
head was filled with the marvelous images and memories
that the word "home" conjured up.

Minmei opened her eyes, recalling that the restraint
was the fanliner's seat belt. Behind her, the steady vibra-
tion of the propfan engine drove them along. "Look!"
Rick said, pointing.

"Mount Fuji!" she shrilled, happy beyond words. The
mountain wore a crown of snow despite the fact that it
was midsummer—something that happened very rarely.
Minmei took it as a good omen and a welcome home.

Rick cruised slowly past Fuji, giving Minmei a chance to look. Air traffic was being rerouted to give him an unobstructed course; he wondered again what secret deals had been struck just so Minmei could see her relatives and wondered too how soon the Macross City survivors would lose patience with their confinement.

He banked the little aircraft, heading for Yokohama. Though he was happy that Minmei would soon have the joy of reunion, he was despondent that their time alone together was nearly half over. He tried to picture her family and how they would react to their daughter's status as SDF-1 superstar.

He trimmed the ship and shook his head. *There are billions of people on this planet. Why did I have to fall in love with public property?*

He took on a bit of altitude; the island chain lay beneath them like so many gemstones.

In the deepest vaults of the Alaskan base, Lisa Hayes and Henry Gloval sat at a simple, unadorned desk in the middle of a vast hearing chamber. The walls of the chamber were several dozen yards thick; though the pressures of the Earth itself were enormous down there, the room itself was as comfortable, in terms of temperature and air pressure, as any surface garden.

There was a multimedia console, perhaps ten yards away, at the base of the wall before them, and all around were display screens as big as billboards. Lisa and Gloval were still arranging documents and papers on the table, preparing to give their testimony.

Though he said nothing about it and gave no outward sign, Lisa knew that Captain Gloval was absolutely furious. He and his First Officer had been denied the courtesy of a face-to-face meeting with Earth's governing body and had been shown, instead, to this interrogation chamber.

Lisa knew he didn't blame her, but she couldn't meet his eye. She knew that her own father was one of those responsible for this shameful, cowardly treatment.

Suddenly all the screens came to life. There were a half dozen extremely magnified faces glaring down Lisa and her captain. All the faces were male, middle-aged to elderly, and all but two were in military uniform.

It confirmed Gloval's worst misgivings. Lisa had to remind herself to breathe. *Military running the government? This wasn't what we were fighting for!*

Before her, on the center screen, was the towering face of her father.

"Welcome home, Captain Gloval," said Admiral Hayes. "It's been a long time since you reported in person."

Gloval snapped his hand to his forehead in salute, and Lisa followed suit. Others might forget their vows, their obligations; but the one thing that sustained Gloval was the certainty that while he still lived he would never renege on his sworn word. Even if it meant rendering military courtesies to men he no longer respected.

It was a code of conduct few outsiders could have understood; a samurai maybe. Gloval had understood and willingly accepted his oath of allegiance to the new United Earth Government, back when the alternative was racial annihilation. He meant to live up to that oath just as long as he was able.

So he rendered military courtesy crisply.

"Yes, sir," replied Henry Gloval.

The huge eyes of the projected image, as blue as Lisa's, turned to her. "You too, Commander."

"Yes, Admiral," she said quietly. She gave no outward sign that her heart was breaking.

After her mother's death, her father had been her only emotional mainstay, until Karl Riber and, later, Claudia, Captain Gloval, and a very few others. And now, Admiral Hayes didn't even deign to break formality. An embrace and a few tears weren't military, perhaps, but she'd hoped for them; and, to be sure, she'd come prepared with some of her own.

But instead, the screen face said, "Good. Now, why don't you both have a seat and we'll hear your report?"

"Yes, sir." Lisa and Gloval cut their salutes away smartly, precise and correct. They both sat while Lisa gathered her briefing data, then she stood again. Gloval felt a sudden burn, since she would have to bear the brunt of their inquiry. But the structure of the meeting was traditional and dictated by custom: The First Officer made the presentation because the Captain was sacrosanct and not subject to cross-examination outside of a court-martial.

"We must know everything from the beginning," said a white-haired man with a snowy handlebar moustache. He was a former political hack who had oiled his way into a direct commission in the Judge Advocate General's office and made his rise from there. Lisa took one look at the ribbons on his tunic and knew he had never seen a single moment of combat.

She had two decorations for courage under fire as well as numerous other campaign ribbons and medals, but she bit her lip and said, "Of course, sir."

Lisa arranged the papers in her hands and looked straight into the image of her father's face. He didn't look away. All around her were august visages; it was like being in an observatory with televisor screens running from floor to ceiling apex.

Lisa gazed at her father coldly.

"This report presumes that everyone present is familiar with the details of the situation up to the time of the Zentraedi's appearance in the solar system. Supplementary reports will be made available to you."

She glared at her father for a second, then went back to her report, happy that Gloval was at her side but ashamed of her own family. She turned instead to a commissioner whose face was displayed to her right, a man who looked like Clark Kent in those ancient *Superman* comics.

She cleared her throat, looked at the overbearing faces around her, and suddenly felt strong; strong as only people with simple truth and dedication to duty on their side can feel. She could stand up to any of them.

"The following are the abbreviated details of the miscalculated spacefold jump undertaken by the Super Dimensional Fortress One while under unprecedentedly intense attack from hostile alien forces and its consequent actions in returning to Terra."

That was quite a mouthful, but Lisa took pride in how fascinated and *intimidated* those enormous, concave faces looked.

These were men who had used the emergency of the Zentraedi's appearance to take control of Earth. Along the way they had evidently forgotten how terrible and overwhelming the enemy was that currently prowled the dark beyond their tiny planet.

Lisa let herself feel a little vindictive; she figured they had it coming. "At that time, the strength of the alien fleet was estimated at nearly one million ships of a size three or more times larger than our Terran Armor class," she said with a certain relish.

And before anybody could say anything, Lisa Hayes added, as she stared her father in the eye, "That number has since increased and our best intelligence evaluations indicate the Zentraedi committment to this war to be in excess of two and a half million ships-of-the-line."

Nobody said anything, but there was clearly a mental echo running round the sad little rabbit hole of the United Earth rulers: *TWO AND A HALF MILLION SHIPS???!*

Chew on that! Lisa thought to herself as she went on to the next page, watching out of one eye as the great and the mighty of Earth squirmed in their seats.

* * *

Yokohama was picture-postcard perfect under a blue sky dotted by slender wisps of white cloud.

Minmei tugged Rick along by the hand as they headed for her parents' restaurant. She stopped in the middle of the esplanade, looking out at the glittering ocean.

"Just smell that beautiful sea air!" She drew in a great breath of it. "*Nothing* smells as good as Yokohama!"

She took her hands from the guardrail, went on full point, pirouetted, and then did a few jetés. "It makes me want to sing, and dance, and *carry on!*"

Rick, trying not to feel like a secret agent but aware of his responsibility, caught her by the upper arm. "Minmei, would you please stop acting like this? Everybody's looking at you."

Shaking off his grip, she spun on him, putting her face up to his furiously. "Listen, I'm happy to be home, and if I feel like singing and dancing, *I will*! *Hmmph*!"

Rick was about to mention their obligation to the SDF-1 and the secrecy to which they'd *both* been sworn for this mission, when Minmei spied a tall, slender structure nearby.

"Look! There's the New Yokohama Marine Tower!" she squealed, pointing down the esplanade. She took on the reserved voice of the tour guides she'd heard so often while she was growing up.

"'When it was built, the New Marine Tower, which replaced the first, was the tallest structure in the world; over twenty-eight hundred feet high! It's an engineering masterpiece.'"

She did another jeté. "It's the same age as me!"

Rick's patience was fading. He doubted that the tower had very much longer to live if its life expectancy was tied in to Minmei's.

"It looks it," he commented.

She thumped him hard on the chest with her fist.

"Doesn't anything impress you, Rick Hunter? I want you to *like* my city!"

It was another one of Minmei's masterful emotional flip-flops: She won him over again in a single moment, as he stared into those enormous blue eyes while she tossed her head, sending ripples of light through her jet-dark hair.

Does she know she has this effect, or is it all unconscious? he wondered. He'd never dared ask the question.

She had her hand in his. "I just *know* you're going to like my mother! She's the nicest, friendliest woman in the whole world! Rick, I'm not kidding!"

She tugged him along. "Come on!"

Who am I to resist? he thought, yielding to the inevitable.

A few minutes later, they came to a *torii* that spanned the street, inscribed with ideographs. "Hey, this is the local Chinatown!" Rick remarked.

Minmei shook her head in dismay; how could such a brilliant pilot be so dumb about other things? "I know, silly. *I'm* Chinese; this is where I live. Come on; let's go!"

She grabbed his hand again and dragged him along, under the *torii* and into Chinatown.

People stared at them a bit, curious about the trim young man in the circus flier's outfit and the enchanting young woman who seemed to radiate life and exuberance. "Now, the grocery store is right over there," Minmei was saying, "right next to the gift shop. And the bakery is still—Rick, have you ever tasted mandarin root? Oh, and I'm *so* glad they haven't changed the street signs!"

The signs were in the shape of smaller *torii.* "You haven't been gone *that* long," he reminded her. What did she expect? Funeral bunting on every corner?

"Right," she said, barely having heard him. "I hope my house is still the same. Just a minute now..."

He'd stopped as she slowed to a halt.

"Look!" She was pointing to a building facade covered with ideographs and intertwined symbols, gold on scarlet, with a very conspicuous dragon in the midst of it. "We're here!"

She turned to Rick excitedly, and he found himself returning her smile in spite of himself. "It's the Golden Dragon, our restaurant, see? Just like the White Dragon is Aunt Lena's in Macross!"

"It's very nice," was all Rick could find to say.

Minmei was close to tears of joy. "I hope everybody remembers my face."

Rick sighed. "I keep trying to tell you, you haven't been gone that long!"

"So? Maybe I've changed a lot." She struck a pose; he recognized it from her glamour photos and feared the worst.

Minmei gave a carefree laugh and went dashing into the Golden Dragon. With no alternative, Rick followed after.

"Chang! Chang!" she was shouting into the face of a startled and rather nervous-looking Chinese gentleman dressed in a white waiter's tunic and matching Nehru hat. "D' you recognize me? Look! Who am I?" She twirled before him.

Chang, his eyes the size of poker chips, said something in a language Rick didn't recognize and charged off into the kitchen, crying, "Look! Come look, come look!"

He was back in a moment, dragging a brown-haired, kind-faced woman whose features bore a resemblance to Minmei's. "Chang, why are you shoving me? What in the world—stop pushing—*oh*!"

"Don't *you* recognize me, Mother?"

She had spied Minmei and stopped, wordless—perhaps close to cardiac arrest.

"Does that mean you do?" Minmei smiled.

"Minmei . . . we were sure you'd been killed!"

"No; I'm home," she said brightly.

Minmei's mother rushed over to throw her arms

around her daughter, nearly knocking her down. "I can't believe it! My darling little girl is home! She wasn't taken from us!" She was racked with sobs.

"Well, I *was*, really," Minmei said, pulled a little off balance by her mother's tight embrace around her neck. "But they brought me back."

Her mother suddenly had her at arm's length again. "Back from where? And who's this?"

"This is Rick Hunter, Mother. He's the boy who saved my life."

Minmei's mother suddenly clasped Rick's hand, bowing over it solemnly, again and again. "Thank you; thank you, son!"

Rick scratched his head with his free hand, not knowing what to say. Among other things, he wasn't at all sure he liked being referred to as a "boy"—especially by the young woman he cared for so much.

"Minmei! We thought you were dead!" A thick-bodied, angry-looking man had appeared from the kitchen. He had dark eyes and hair as black as his daughter's.

"How could you not contact us and let us know you were alive?" But even though he was scowling, her father touched her face tenderly.

Meanwhile, Rick was having some very troubling thoughts of his own. The G2 Security officers who had briefed him for this oddball mission had been very emphatic that he not discuss any details of the situation on the SDF-1; even Minmei had agreed to be circumspect about revealing any information about the vessel or its mission.

But these people behaved as if the ship had been lost with all hands even though it had been back for over twenty-four hours now.

Rick took the briefing officers' instructions to heart, deciding to say as little as possible—and to see that Minmei did the same, though that promised to be a chore—until he had a clearer idea of just what was going on here on Earth.

CHAPTER
TWELVE

*Gloval's ship and crew had been tested in the flame and
come through. The Robotechnology and the civilian refugees, likewise, had undergone a make-or-break trial.*

*No one had foreseen that an even more severe strain was
to be put on Gloval's own oath of allegiance.*

"The Second Front," *History of the First Robotech
War*, Vol. LXVI.

THE GIANT FACE OF A COUNCIL MEMBER LOOKED
down at Lisa as she set down her briefing book, her sum-
mary complete.

"That was a very comprehensive report, Commander
Hayes," the Council member, General Herbert, said.
"But come now, don't you think you've overestimated
the enemy's strength by quite a lot?"

Herbert disappeared, and the image of Marshal
Zukav, silver-haired and silver-mustached, took its
place. "Yes, I can't help but wonder why these aliens
didn't destroy the battle fortress if they had such over-
whelmingly superior numbers."

Lisa, who'd seated herself, came to her feet again.
Gloval said nothing, glaring up at the magnified faces
around him, content to let his First Officer draw out the

Council's attitudes and arguments before he made his stand.

"I've already stated what we believe to be their motives in my report."

Herbert was back. "You expect us to accept that report as the truth?"

Lisa growled, gritting her teeth, her hands bunching into fists, trying to keep her temper.

Then her father, Admiral Hayes, was staring down at her. "That will be all, Commander; we've heard quite enough. You may resume your seat."

"Admiral, I—"

But Gloval was on his feet now, with a calming hand on her shoulder. She held her peace.

"Gentlemen," he addressed the Council, "what about the authorization for the requests that were attached to that report?"

Now Zukav glared down at him again. "The proposal to negotiate with the enemy and the plans to relocate the Macross City survivors?"

Herbert broke in, "We will discuss your requests in private session. You and your First will stand by!" There was a loud comtone, and all screens went blank, leaving Lisa and Gloval in a sudden silence in the dim, domed chamber.

Lisa's fists were trembling. "Ohhhh! I can't *believe* they treated us like this!"

Gloval lowered himself into his chair, head thrown back, eyes closed. "I do. I think we've lost the fight."

"But—how can you know that already?"

"There's something going on here that we don't know about, Lisa. Their minds are made up."

She gazed around at the darkened screens. "I wonder what they're planning to do with us?"

Minmei's father slammed his fist on the table, making the teacups jump. "No! You're *not* going!"

"That's right!" her mother added. "After more than a

year we finally discover that you're not dead; how can you think we'd let you leave?"

"To go entertain troops on some warship." Her father sneered.

Minmei was on her feet, hands on hips. "Hah! Is that what you think I'm doing?" She stamped one little foot. "I'm not just some run-of-the-mill USO singer, you know! I'm an important person back there!"

Her father shouted, "Well, you're *not* back there! You're *here*, and I'm not letting you return, and that's that!"

She threw her head back, eyes squeezed shut, shaking her fists. *"No-o-o-o!"* Then she went on. "I've *got* to go back! I'm doing a TV show, I've got a record coming out, and I'm going to be starring in a film! Isn't that right, Rick?"

Rick was completely taken by surprise at the sudden shift of focus to him. "Uh, um—"

"Ridiculous! Your family comes first!" her father barked.

Rick was wondering about that, too. When he and Minmei were stranded, she had talked at length about all the love and mutual support there was in her family. It looked like a little celebrity could change a *lot* of things.

"I want to be a movie star!" she pouted, stamping both feet this time, just as her cousin Jason did when he threw a tantrum.

Her mother was weeping into a snow-white napkin. "How could you hurt us like this? You know we've always counted on you to get married and take over the Golden Dragon and run it with your husband."

Married? Run the restaurant? *Those* were new wrinkles! Rick suddenly felt a little queasy at the very thought of giving up flying, even for Minmei. Maybe they weren't destined for each other, after all.

"What about you, young man?" her father snapped. "What d' you think about all this hogwash, eh?"

"Huh? That is—well—"

Minmei was furious. "I don't see why you're asking him! His opinion doesn't count here! I'm the one making the decision! It's my life, and I'm going back to the ship; I can't turn my back on thousands of loyal fans and all the people I work with!"

Her mother sniffed and said, "But you're turning your back on us."

Score one for Mom, Rick thought; that shot had hit home, stopping Minmei in her tracks, at least for the moment.

But just when she might have yielded, a new voice interrupted. "Hey, what's all the screaming about down here? I can't even concentrate on my studies—hey! Minmei!"

He was about Rick's age or a little older, tall, with straight hair as black as Minmei's that fell past his shoulders. He'd stepped down out of the stairway—a slim, athletic-looking fellow, handsome but somehow sullen. Still, his face lit up when he saw her.

She flew to him, hugging herself to him. "Kyle! Oh, I can't believe it! You're *here*! I thought I'd never see you again!"

He laughed and held her close.

She spoke in a flurry. "We thought you died on Macross! We never found you in the shelters, or later on the SDF-1, so your parents and I assumed—"

He shrugged. "After my father kicked me out of the house for being in the peace movement, I figured it wasn't such a good idea to stick around a military town. So I left the day before Launching Day."

Rick was looking at him jealously. Kyle had a sort of inner balance, a calmness—unflappable and very self-possessed.

"When I tried to get in touch with you," he was telling Minmei, "they told me that everything on the island had been destroyed and that it was off limits for good. Radioactive or something." His face clouded with the memory, a sensitive and strong face.

"It was terrible." She nodded sadly.

He took her shoulders. "Well, I'm glad *you're* here; I'm glad *somebody* survived."

"Oh, but your mom and dad are doing just fine, running the White Dragon!"

"What?" His grip tightened on her shoulders for a moment, powerful fingers digging in until he realized what he was doing and eased off. "They're alive?"

She gave him a smile warm as a hearth fire. "Sure, silly; they're on the ship."

"Ship? What're you taking about?"

She *tch*ed and explained, "The *space*ship."

"You mean you didn't know?" Rick asked, wondering just how much covering up he was going to have to do.

Kyle was shaking his head happily, baffled but laughing. "No."

"Most of us survived, even though we lost a lot of people," Minmei told him. "This is Lieutenant Rick Hunter; he's one of the fighter pilots from the ship."

Kyle said, "Oh. Hello." It sounded like he was greeting the lowest known life form.

Rick rose anyway, trying to be polite. "Hi."

"Rick," Minmei gushed, "this is my cousin Lynn-Kyle; he's been like a brother to me. Kyle, Rick is the one who saved my life."

"It was a privilege." Rick shrugged.

Kyle's expression was full of anger and resentment. "I thought soldiers were *expected* to aid civilians in times of emergency."

Rick cocked his head to one side, trying to figure out what Kyle's beef was. "Hmmm."

"But we appreciate your efforts, anyway," Kyle told him with a frown.

Minmei slipped an arm through Kyle's elbow. "No, no: When Rick saved my life, he hadn't *become* a soldier yet."

Kyle was looking him up and down with narrowed eyes. "So you decided to join up later, eh?"

Minmei's mother and father were watching the whole exchange without interfering; Rick wondered just what he'd gotten into the middle of. "That's right."

Kyle held his chin high, gazing down his nose at Rick. "What d' you think's so good about the military?"

Rick showed his teeth in a snarling smile. "Free bullets, free food . . . and it sure beats *working* for a living."

"It's getting late," Gloval said grimly just as a comtone sounded.

Hours had gone by. In the interview chamber at the bottom of the Alaskan base, the screens flashed to life again. Gloval and Lisa looked up expectantly, wondering what the result of the deliberation was. The wall clock read nearly midnight.

General Herbert gazed down at them. "Captain, Commander—sorry to keep you waiting." He didn't sound sorry at all. "The Council has been going over your report, and we have found most of it to be accurate."

"And what about my requests?"

"Captain Gloval, all negotiations with the aliens for an end to hostilities are flatly rejected."

Gloval spat, "You think we can win against a force like that?"

"We don't know whether we can win or not. The point is, we don't understand the invaders' thinking. We scarcely understand their Robotechnology. How can we begin peace talks with them?"

Gloval was about to interrupt, but Herbert pushed on. "We have no way of knowing if they would participate in good faith or simply ignore any treaty commitments and attack again when it suited them."

"But—you must realize—" Gloval began.

Then Admiral Hayes's image was front and center. "Captain, we think our Grand Cannon will protect us as long as we stay prepared and alert. We will *not* negotiate away that advantage."

"Very well," Gloval snapped. "I understand, sir. But

what about resettling the fifty thousand or so Macross survivors?"

Herbert fielded that one, seeming irked that he would even ask the question. "They've all been declared dead, so having them leave the SDF-1 is out of the question, Gloval."

Gloval shook his head slowly. "I don't understand."

Lisa shot to her feet. "Just what is it you're saying?"

Herbert's answer was acid. "Do you think we made an official announcement that we're at war with *aliens*? Why, there would have been worldwide panic and probable insurrection by the peace factions!"

"They'd have been screaming for immediate unconditional surrender," another Council member, Commissioner Blaine of US-Western, added.

Admiral Hayes's image held the center spot again. "We invoked a strict media blackout from the day the SDF-1 disappeared, using the excuse that a guerrilla force of antiunification terrorists had attacked Macross Island and destroyed it after the ship left on its maiden test flight. Now, how could we let the tens of thousands of Macross inhabitants who *know* what a tremendous threat we face return to Earth?"

"It's impossible!" Zukav threw in. "The government would be overthrown!"

Are they crazy or am I? Gloval asked himself.

For ten years, throughout the rebuilding of SDF-1, the world government had used the threat of alien invasion to justify their staggering defense budgets and its own ever-expanding influence.

But when the Zentraedi finally appeared with power so far beyond anything humans had envisioned (except for a few hardheaded realists like Gloval), the Council had, in effect, become completely paranoid: They lied to the populace, hid in a hole in the ground, and simply prayed the menace would go away.

All for the sake of their political power base, all so that they could rule a little longer.

Gloval's voice rose a few decibels. "We're going to have a riot on our hands if we don't allow those people to get off the ship! They've been through a lot and endured it gallantly, but now they're safely back home and their patience is wearing thin!"

Herbert answered that. "Keeping them under control is your responsibility. And anyway, if, as you stated in your report, the aliens are so curious about our customs, then carrying an entire city within the SDF-1 should ensure that their attention is focused on it, don't you think?"

"It's crucial that you draw the enemy forces away from this planet!" Kinsolving, a bloodless-looking man with eyes like glass pellets, said from one side.

"At what price?" Gloval roared.

He felt very close to surrendering to his rage—perhaps going back to the SDF-1 and launching a little revolution of his *own*.

But he knew he wouldn't, knew he couldn't fire on innocent men and women who believed the Council's lies and who would rise to oppose him—knew he couldn't break the oath of allegiance he'd sworn.

He'd seen enough civil war; he knew he couldn't start another.

Admiral Hayes was saying, "Captain, we're not insensitive to your situation, but we must have time to strengthen our defenses and increase our knowledge of Robotechnology. And you're the only one who can give it to us."

Lisa cried, "Father, this is too much to ask of all those civilians!"

Hayes's huge projected face glared down at her icily. "Commander Hayes, we may be father and daughter, but during these proceedings I expect to be addressed by my rank, is that understood?"

"Yes, sir," she spit out the words.

"And what if the aliens decide not to follow the battle fortress?" Gloval posed the question. "What if they attack the Earth instead? You can fire your Grand Cannon until you broil away the planet's atmosphere and make the surrounding land mass run molten, but you *still* won't be able to destroy all those ships!"

Hayes answered, "Your own analysis indicates that that's highly unlikely; the invaders are interested in your ship. You will receive your sailing orders in the morning. That is all."

Again the screens went blank.

Gloval picked up his hat tiredly. *I guess that's the end of that.*

"Captain, how are we ever going to be able to explain this to the people on the ship? Not just the survivors; the crew—they've been in constant combat for more than a year!"

Gloval had no answer. In the corridor outside, he asked, "Lisa, wouldn't you like to spend some time with your father while you're here? As family, I mean? I can authorize a brief leave . . ."

They came to an elevator to begin the long trip back to the surface. Lisa kept her eyes lowered to the floor. "No, sir. I have no particular interest in seeing him right now."

"I understand, my dear," said Gloval as the elevator doors closed.

CHAPTER
THIRTEEN

> *The patterns of behavior observed so far indicate that either all these humans are demented or else the three of us suffered head injuries upon first landing here.*
>
> Preliminary observation of the Zentraedi spies Rico, Bron, and Konda

I REALLY DON'T THINK THIS IS GETTING US ANY-where," Lynn-Kyle said in his soft, reasonable voice.

Hours of argument had gone by, but the five—Minmei and her parents, Rick, and Lynn-Kyle—were still gathered around the table. "Minmei's made her decision," Kyle went on, "so why don't you let her go?"

Minmei clapped her hands, eyes dancing. "Oh, Kyle, you're wonderful! I knew you'd say that!"

"Just a minute!" Minmei's father said angrily.

His wife was quick to head off the brewing confrontation with Kyle and keep the debate on track. "You're the last one we'd expect to send Minmei away from her home, Kyle."

"Especially with no one to watch over her," the father added. Rick almost said something about that: *Listen, I saved her from fifty-foot-tall aliens and death by starva-*

tion and thirst! What d' ya call that, a passing interest?
But it didn't seem like the time.

"I thought I would go with her," Kyle said casually,
"and live with my folks."

Minmei was ecstatic. "Hurray, Lynn-Kyle! I knew
you'd find some way to come to my rescue!"

Rick made a bored sound.

"Well, I guess that's all right," Lynn-Jan said slowly,
deciding it might be for the best to let his daughter get this
foolishness out of her system. His wife, Lynn-Xian, looked
relieved, saying, "It would make me feel a lot better."

"No problem," Kyle said with a charming smile. "It's
just temporary, anyway."

The transport hurtled through the frigid night air,
bound for the SDF-1. A full squadron of fighters was
flying escort around it.

Gloval knew now that it was no longer a matter of
honor; he wouldn't be given the chance to divert or dis-
obey orders now that the Council had made its decision.

Lisa, sitting in the window seat, opened an envelope
that one of her father's aides had given to her. She read:

My dearest Lisa,
   I know that you're angry about my decision re-
garding the SDF-1, but it was unavoidable under
the circumstances. I want you to try to understand
and realize I'm concerned about your welfare. The
battle fortress is a very dangerous place, and I'm
working on getting you reassigned to another ship,
or possibly here to headquarters, before it's or-
dered to move out into space once more—

Without finishing the note, she tore it into tiny little
pieces.

From another direction, the speedy little fanliner cut
the sky, bound for the ship. It was handling a little less

nimbly than before; Lynn-Kyle was seated in the back with Minmei in his lap.

"You mean to say you don't have *any* girlfriends?" she was asking him coquettishly, batting those big blue eyes.

He looked at her fondly, but he seemed to be one of the few people immune to her manipulation. "Well, I've been traveling around so much, I haven't had time."

"If you *did* have a girlfriend, I'd probably be jealous."

He chuckled. "What d' you have in mind? You want me to stay single forever?"

"Well, not exactly," she said slyly.

It sounded like a game they'd played often, Rick thought. "Then what *do* you want?" Kyle coaxed.

She knuckled his shoulders, giggling. "Oh, nothing; I'm just teasing."

Rick lost patience with all the cuteness; he couldn't take any more of it. "Hey! It's hard enough to fly this crate, overloaded like this, without all that jabbering back there! How about buttoning up until we land?"

He was also bothered by the idea that he might have exceeded orders. There were no provisions for him to bring an outsider aboard the SDF-1; but, on the other hand, the briefing officers were very emphatic that Minmei was important to the war effort and must be returned, and Minmei couldn't come back without Kyle, so . . .

Minmei was giggling again. "That boy's always kidding," she confided to Kyle.

That tears it! "Guess again," he told her. "It's no joke!"

He banked sharply; Minmei let out a squeal and clung closer to Kyle. Rick poured on the speed, impatient to be rid of the two of them.

Lynn-Kyle held his cousin close and smiled triumphantly.

* * *

"That's not fair!" Kim Young cried, hearing Gloval's heartbreaking news.

"It's like we're prisoners here!" Sammie added.

Gloval stood his ground, unmoving, betraying no emotion. He'd thought it best to let his trusted bridge crew in on the news first, in the privacy of the bridge; they were the ones who would form the core of what he was coming to think of as his crisis-management team, helping him ensure that things didn't fall apart aboard SDF-1. They had to be given time to get over the shock before they could help the entire ship's population cope with it.

Claudia was the first one to get things in perspective. "Orders are orders, even if there are a lot of idiots at central headquarters who have no idea what they're doing!"

Lisa nodded to herself; she *knew* that was the kind of woman and officer Claudia was.

Still, Sammie insisted, "But there must be *something* you can do, Captain. Please tell us you're not going to accept this quietly. You will change their minds, won't you?"

"Won't you, Captain?" Kim added pleadingly.

Gloval cleared his throat in the way he did when he'd heard enough and expected to be obeyed. "Your lack of discipline is only compounding the problem, so get back to your duty stations immediately. I appreciate your concern, but right now I have to begin deciding how to break the news to the Macross survivors and the rest of the crew."

He stood up from his chair, brushing past them. "You will excuse me."

Shifting her glasses nervously, Vanessa couldn't help calling a last desperate objection after him. "Captain, can't you—"

Gloval cut her off stiffly. "That will be all, Vanessa."

"Yes, sir," she said contritely.

"Try to understand," Gloval said softly over his shoulder to them just before the hatch closed.

Vanessa removed her glasses to wipe away a tear of anger. "But—it's not fair!"

"That's absolutely true," Lisa said, speaking up for the first time. "But you can't blame the captain for something headquarters did. Everybody has a right to gripe, but you should at least be mad at the right people."

"Okay, okay—the captain needs our support, right?" Claudia said soberly.

"Yes. He knows he can't possibly succeed without it," Lisa answered.

The bridge hatch opened, and the relief watch started filing in. Kim let her breath go with a rasp. "All this talk isn't going to change anything, and I'm hungry," she declared, careful to mention nothing specific in the outsiders' presence.

Sammie took the cue. "Let's go into town and eat lunch!"

Vanessa nodded energetically. "Yeah, let's go down to the White Dragon; I'm starving."

At the White Dragon, the front doors slid aside. Minmei's aunt Lena quickly went to greet the first customers of the lunch rush, bowing hospitably. The restaurant was braced for a busy day; people were boisterous, in a mood to continue their celebrating even though a lot of them were getting restless and edgy with the delay in disembarkation.

It didn't disturb her husband Max very much; "People will always have to eat," was his motto. But Lena knew a certain sadness. In spite of the dreadful things the SDF-1 and Macross had gone through, the rebuilt restaurant held a wealth of happy memories.

"Welcome," she said, "welc—*oh*!"

A ghost had come through the door, surrounded by a cloud of brilliance from the brighter EVE "sunlight."

Her hands flew to her mouth. "Oh, Kyle, is it really you?"

He took a step closer. In the well-remembered, soft, clear voice, he said gently, "Yes, Mother; I'm home. And I've missed you very much."

Dimly, she was aware of the traffic passing by on the street outside and of Minmei and Rick Hunter waiting a few paces back. Minmei was barely keeping herself from weeping. Rick was straightfaced, showing no emotion; but he envied the Lynn family their connectedness and their warmth, Minmei's tantrums notwithstanding.

When he thought about it, Rick realized that the closest thing he had to family was Roy Fokker and—to a slightly lesser extent—his wingmen, Max and Ben. So Rick endeavored not to think of it.

Lena walked haltingly to her son. "Kyle, is this a dream? I can hardly believe my eyes! Oh, my baby!" She cupped his face in her hands.

"No, it's not a dream, Mother; it's me."

Tears rolled down her cheeks. "I've missed you so." Lena threw herself into his arms.

"Gee," Minmei said, wiping away moisture from her eyes. "I'm so happy, I'm gonna cry."

Lena truly noticed Rick and her niece for the first time. "Oh, dear! This is no way to welcome you two home!"

Minmei was snuffling and sobbing openly now. "Aw, don't worry about us," Rick said.

Lena said, "Now, now; come in!" She kept her hold on her son's shoulders as he took another step into the White Dragon. Minmei had assured him that in virtually every detail it was an exact duplicate of the old place, the one that had been destroyed on Macross Island. But this was astounding!

There was a clatter of bowls and a rattle of chopsticks over by the pickup counter. Lynn-Kyle essayed another of his gentle smiles. "Father. I've missed you, too. You're looking well."

Max snorted gruffly, looking the boy over. Gathering the last of the bowls with an irritated grunt, he vanished back into the kitchen.

Lena went to plead with him. "Now, dear! *Please* don't be so—"

But Kyle had caught her wrist, pulling her back. "Mother, don't get upset, I beg you. Father's always been that way around me, you know that."

Washing up the last of the dishes, Max scarcely knew what he was doing; his mind was far away, on the years and the rift between himself and his son. "I always knew he'd come back," he muttered to himself, words drowned out by the jetting water and the other sounds of the kitchen. "No alien sneak attack could've killed *him*."

He had to stop, to dry his eyes and blow his nose. "What else could I think? He *is* my son."

And he couldn't help but surrender to the proud smile he'd kept hidden.

The three Zentraedi spies crouched before the display window of a sushi and tempura shop not far away, gazing hungrily at the appetizing dishes there. Their mouths watered, and their jaws ached with hunger. Rico's face and hands were pressed flat against the glass.

"So d' you suppose that stuff is food?" Konda asked aloud.

Bron had a hypnotized grin on his face, eyes never leaving the display. "Mmm, well, *something* sure smells good here, and I'm getting pretty hungry."

The tiny supply of concentrate capsules they'd brought with them was long gone, and they hadn't eaten since the free food at the party on *Daedalus*'s flight deck the day before.

The other two made ravenous sounds of agreement. Thus far, they hadn't been able to figure out how to requisition food on the SDF-1; Macross City was filled with an astounding variety of things, all of which seemed to change hands through a system based on pieces of paper.

But how to get the paper? The humans' system of distribution and ration allocation seemed the maddest thing of all about their society.

The three took a few steps back to stare in fascination at the window and consider their problem. "So who's goin' in to get our rations?" Konda posed the question.

"That's easy," replied Bron, hitching his belt up. "I'll go."

"No, *I'll* go!" Rico insisted. Before the other two could raise the question of tactics, the smallest spy backed up a few steps and, with a running start, slammed his shoulder into the plate glass.

The glass heaved and shattered, pieces of it raining down inside the display case and out on the sidewalk. By some chance, Rico wasn't hurt at all.

The owner, a sturdy-looking woman in her forties wearing flat slippers and an apron over her working clothes, came charging out onto the sidewalk. She held a heavy, long-handled ladle in one formidable-looking fist.

"Hey, what's going on out here— Oh!" She watched dumbfounded as Rico, squatting on his haunches, claimed his right as winner of the food and had the first portion. Konda and Bron were looking on avidly.

But Rico spit out the stuff that was in his mouth and spit again, making horrible faces. "Inedible! *Plaugh!*"

She shook her ladle at him. "What's wrong with you? Of *course* it's not food. Don't you know the difference between real food and a plastic window display?"

She took a step toward him, and Rico fell over backward on the seat of his pants, intimidated by the implement she held—from the confidence she showed, it was obviously a lethal weapon, perhaps a Robotech device. Konda and Bron skipped back, ready to do battle but more inclined to run from such a fearsome opponent.

She set her hands on her hips, looking down at Rico, who waited miserably to be set upon and wounded or killed. But she said, "If you're trying to eat that, I guess you really *must* be hungry."

She'd thought that arrangements for feeding everyone in the SDF-1 had missed nothing, but perhaps these three loonies were a special case—incapable of coping with even the least contact with bureaucracy. There were always going to be those who fell through the social safety net, she decided, even on the SDF-1.

She wasn't the kind to let people go hungry, and what's more, she was filled with the joy of the return to Earth and the promised end to her hardships. She pointed to the door of her restaurant.

"C'mon inside, you three, and I'll fix you something to eat. And I mean *real* food!"

She went inside, and the three spies looked at one another.

"She's going to give us food? Just like that?" Bron said blankly. "Just because she sees we're hungry?"

"How can a chaotic system like this possibly function?" Konda wondered, rubbing his jaw.

"I don't care, just as long as it functions for another half hour or so!" proclaimed Rico, scrambling to his feet.

It was insane, against all logic. And yet, knowing how it felt to be very, very hungry and have someone act toward them in this absurd but *very* welcome manner, they had to admit that there was something about it— something admirable. Something that struck a chord deep within them.

It was completely unlike the Zentraedi; it even smacked of a kind of weakness. But it stirred up new and confusing response patterns.

"Hey, wait for us!" Rico yelped, scuttling along after her. Konda and Bron crowded each other for second place.

CHAPTER
FOURTEEN

*In recent years, Karl Riber hadn't come so often to mind
—not more than once or twice a day, sometimes.*

*Occasionally, I wonder why I stayed in the service, since
it was war that took us apart, war that had made peace-loving Karl volunteer for duty on the Mars Sara Base, that got
him killed in that raid.*

*I was only a teenager, and a rather young one, when he
left. When he died, I thought someday the pain would go
away, the years would wear it out. I know better now.*

Lisa Hayes, *Recollections*

LISA AND HER WATCHMATES SHOWED UP AT THE
White Dragon with Max Sterling bringing up the rear.
Max knew that Rick claimed to dislike them, especially
Commander Hayes; but Max didn't share his feelings.

He even suspected that Rick protested too much, was
too loud in his denunciation of Lisa; Max had seen them
together and knew there was more there than met the
eye, more than either of them was willing to admit. But
far be it from the self-effacing Max Sterling to make any
comment.

As for Kim, Sammie, and Vanessa—the ones Rick
had dubbed the "bridge bunnies"—Max was delighted to
have their company. He thought it good luck to have run
into them and been invited along and figured any VT
jock who wouldn't jump at the chance to have four

good-looking women for company ought to report immediately for a long talk with the flight surgeon.

"Looks kind of crowded, doesn't it?" Kim was saving, just as they realized someone was signaling them. He had a big roundtop all to himself, the only unoccupied table in the place. The bridge bunnies thought it was a sign from providence, and Lisa made no objection to joining him.

"Talk about a case of perfect timing," Rick said as Max ran around trying to hold all the women's chairs at once. "Minmei's long-lost cousin Kyle was in Yokohama. And she wouldn't come back without him."

Lisa's face clouded with disapproval. She knew Rick's orders, and bringing an outsider was tantamount to disobedience. Still, if that was the only way Miss Macross would rejoin the ship, Rick had probably done the right thing, she admitted, even though she couldn't see why the staff people—especially the civilian affairs and morale officers—were so determined that the girl be catered to.

Besides, she knew from her visit to the Alaskan base that there would be no leak of information about the SDF-1's return or Minmei's visit, not even from Minmei's parents. The damned Council gestapo would apply pressure to make sure of that.

"So it's a big reunion," Rick was grousing. "Everybody in the neighborhood came in to see him."

"Gee! What a *hunk*!" Sammie gushed.

Her two cohorts were quick to agree, sounding as if they were about to swoon. Lisa looked over to where Kyle stood with Minmei and his mother, greeting people and exchanging pleasantries with that gentle reserve of his.

Lisa gasped. *He—he reminds me so of Karl!*

Gentle, peace-loving Karl, her one and only love, gone forever.

The Terrible Trio were into their act. "Kim, you shouldn't stare; not so hard!" Sammie giggled.

Kim sniggered back, "Oh, sure! And I suppose *you* saw him *first*?" Sammie dissolved in laughter.

Max seated himself, tossing a forelock of long blue hair out of his eyes, and polished his glasses on his napkin. Vanessa asked Rick, "What did you say her cousin's name was again?"

"I think I said Kyle," Rick grunted.

The Terrible Trio had practiced enough to say it as one, so that everybody in the place could hear: "OH! WELL, HE'S SURE *GOOD-LOOKING*, ISN'T HE?"

Maybe "bridge bunnies" isn't such a bad name for them, after all, Max mused, putting his glasses back on and taking another look at this Lynn-Kyle.

"Gee, Minmei looks so happy," Kim sighed.

Rick had something sour to say on the subject, but at that moment Mayor Tommy Luan sauntered up to the table, his usual effervescent self.

"Well, well, well, Rick, m' boy! So these are some of your friends, eh? Why don't you introduce me to the ladies, hmm?"

Rick wondered if there was ever a time when Tommy Luan *wasn't* campaigning. But before he could comply, Minmei's cousin was there, with Minmei trailing behind like a faithful pet.

"Hello, Mr. Mayor; glad to have you back on Earth. I'd like to introduce myself: My name is Lynn-Kyle. Welcome to my family's restaurant."

Minmei, clinging to his arm, added, "Hi!"

Rick heard a little sound escape Lisa and saw that something about Kyle made her very distraught. The Terrible Trio fell all over one another greeting Kyle, and Max mumbled some adequate response.

The mayor said heartily, "Well, Kyle, even if you don't like the army, you'll have to admit there are some lovely ladies in the military!"

Lisa gasped. He even had the same convictions as Karl!

"Oh, uh, did I say something perhaps I shouldn't

have?" Tommy Luan asked with elaborate innocence. "Well, young people should get to know one another." He sauntered off. "'Scuse me."

Max had the distinct impression that the mayor was wearing a satisfied smirk—as though he'd succeeded at something. But what?

"Was the mayor implying you have something against the service?" Sammie piped up.

Kyle shook his head, the long, straight midnight hair shimmering. "It's not just the military. I don't like fighting of any kind."

Sammie rested her chin on her hands and batted her eyelashes at him. "Oh, really?" For a guy this dreamy, she'd have sat happily listening to him do Zentraedi half-time cheers. Minmei gave Sammie a suspicious scowl.

"Fighting produces nothing!" Kyle declared. "It only results in devastation and destruction!"

Max was studying Kyle with an unusual directness. "Are you saying that everyone in the service enjoys destroying things?"

Rick couldn't help jumping in, even if it offended Minmei. Maybe even because it would. "Well, *I* didn't join the Robotech Defense Forces because I like devastation and destruction."

Divine as Lynn-Kyle might be, even the Terrible Trio had to nod and murmur their agreement with that. Minmei intervened, afraid that things were about to get out of control.

"Hey, relax, everybody! We're celebrating Kyle's return, after all. I've got it: They're broadcasting that show I taped yesterday. What about turning on the television?"

That met with general acclaim; if Minmei was the darling and idol of the SDF-1, she was an empress among her friends and neighbors. In another moment the six-foot screen showed her in the center of the spotlights, microphone in hand—not that the sound crew couldn't have used directionals, but she preferred it as a prop. She wore a stunning new Kirstin Hammersjald creation.

The crowd in the White Dragon was cheering and stomping and whistling, as was the crowd in the taping studio. Rick strained to catch a little of the song:

> I spend the days alone,
> Chasing a dream—

All at once the entertainment special disappeared in an avalanche of zigzag static, to be replaced by Colton Van Fortespiel.

Everyone in the SDF-1 knew Van Fortespiel, the SDF Broadcasting System's supervising announcer and the only TV anchorman on record to wear dark wraparound sunglasses on camera. His appearance sent a signal of fear through the room; unscheduled announcements of this sort usually spelled trouble for the dimensional fortress.

For this reason, *and* the sunglasses, Van Fortespiel was sometimes called the Boogieman. The Boogieman was wearing earphones today, too, and speaking into a jumble of mikes that took his voice over the various sound-only circuits, intership comlines, and alternative TV channels.

"We interrupt our regular programming for this very important news bulletin."

The White Dragon resounded with angry resentment. The crowd had felt at home, safe, and had been eagerly watching Minmei; the people wanted no part of any more disaster reports. They were yelling for Minmei's show to be resumed.

"At a news conference moments ago," the Boogieman continued, "Captain Henry Gloval disclosed to the press that permission for any survivors to leave Macross has been denied."

There was a moment of stunned silence as Van Fortespiel shifted his sheets of copy, until a grandmotherly woman howled, "What does he *mean*," 'denied'? Does that mean we're stuck here? For how long?"

Others were raising objections, too, but most were shushing them to hear what else the Boogieman had to say.

"Rumors circulating throughout the ship's upper echelons today indicate that this prohibition may only be temporary."

A man in a brown sport coat shook his fist at the screen and hollered, "We finally make it back to Earth and now they're telling us we have to stay aboard this junk heap?"

A redhaired woman, holding a frightened little girl who wore an RDF insignia on her rompers, wailed, "How much more do they think we can endure? When will all this ever come to an end?"

There were plenty of angry voices to second that. "Yeah; we demand an explanation!" bellowed a guy in a black T-shirt.

But the Boogieman was already returning them to their normally scheduled programming. In another second, Minmei, smiling winsomely in the spotlights, was finishing.

—here by my side!

...and taking a bow. The crowd in the restaurant didn't spare her a clap or a whistle.

Kim murmured, "They spent all that time and *this* was the best announcement they could come up with to break the news?"

Max and Rick traded puzzled, worried looks: *What's she talking about?*

Sammie gulped. "Look, they're not taking it very well. I sure hope this doesn't turn into an all-out rebellion!"

The man in the brown coat said, "Hey, look; we've got those military officers right over there! I say let's get some kind of explanation out of 'em!"

A number of the men there went along with the idea, and in a moment the five RDF members seated at the table found themselves surrounded.

The brown sport coat shook a fist in Rick's face. "C'mon, Lieutenant! Tell us what's goin' on!"

Rick sputtered and stammered, as surprised as anyone. "Well, uh, I guess I don't really know..."

"Stop this!" Lisa snapped. "Stop it right now! How dare you treat us this way? We risked our lives—and plenty of us died!—to get you back here safely!"

Some of the crowd paused at that, but the man in the brown sport coat and a number of others weren't buying it.

"What d' ya want, gratitude?" He sneered. "When we lost everything we had because of your SDF-1? And now you're making us prisoners here?"

He slammed his fist on the table; the Terrible Trio jumped, startled and frightened. "Well? I want a straight answer!"

Lisa tried again, more calmly. "Please, it's just a temporary measure. Just give us—"

He cut her off. "For what, more of the same old promises? We're tired of lies! We're tired of being held here like convicts! Now we take matters into our *own hands*!"

Whoever the brown sport coat was, he was a rabble-rouser of considerable talent. He had almost all the men and quite a few of the women with him, talking about justice and fighting for their rights. And for Lisa the agonizing thing was that she knew that there was a lot to justify their reaction and that her father had been one of those chiefly responsible for doing this to the Macross survivors.

Some loudmouth was yelling, "Why don't we show 'em we mean business? Let's take these punks and *force* 'em to get us off this ship!"

Lisa stood, gathering the others in by eye. "Let's go."

A broken-toothed man clapped a big paw on her shoulder. "Hold it!"

She tried to stare him down. "You'd better let me go."

He shook her. "Siddown!"

But a hand closed on *his* shoulder. "Okay, that's enough."

It was Max Sterling. Rick, halfway out of his chair to help Lisa, did a bit of a double take. Max had been sitting beside him a moment before. *What'd he do,* teleport *over there?*

Max's voice was still mild, but his face showed a certain intensity Rick had seen only during combat. *Look out, tough guy!* Rick thought to the broken-toothed man.

"Take your hand off her. Now."

Max had barely gotten it out when the man threw a punch, screaming, "Shut up!"

Max ducked, but not far. Rick had seen him do this before; Max's incredible reflex time and psychomotor responses let him deal with such things by split seconds and fractions of an inch.

Max avoided the clumsy haymaker and delivered a jolting left, snapping the other's head around, stepping back neatly as he began to collapse.

Other members of what had now become a mob saw what had happened and began to converge on Max, snarling and getting ready to fight.

Max glared at them, unruffled. "You'd better get back."

Somebody shrieked, "Let's get 'em!" and Rick found that he couldn't get to Max because the mob was closing in on *him*, too. A man in a green turtleneck threw a wild left. Rick bobbed under, came up, and planted a solid uppercut, sending him staggering back. Two more men closed in, swinging hastily and inaccurately. He avoided them, backpedaling.

Max was taking on a very muscular young man who had plenty of power but not much style. Max warded off a roundhouse with an inside block, getting a quick hold on that arm. Max's fist went ballistic under the guy's chin, lifting him right off his feet. It was the brawler's good fortune that his tongue was well back in his mouth, or his teeth would have snipped it off.

The muscular one landed sprawling across a table; it crashed down, slamming him on the back of the head as he landed on his butt on the floor.

Lynn-Kyle had neither advanced to help his cousin's friends nor withdrawn from the scene. Rick got one brief look at him: Kyle was standing as rigid and indifferent as a stone idol.

Rick stopped another vigilante with a short, hard shot to the sternum, then rocked him back with a left cross.

Things had gone very well for the two VT pilots up to now, but more and more men were getting ready to wade into the melee as soon as an opening occurred. On the outskirts of things, Lisa and the Terrible Trio were doing what they could. Quite a number of self-appointed public prosecutors never got to mix it up with the pilots because a chop across the neck or a kick to the kneecap put them out of the fight for good.

But the odds against them kept growing. With no chance for a breather and no escape route, Rick and Max knew things would probably swing the other way shortly. There was no helping that, and the brawl had gone too far to be stopped now; they fought on. Rick was accomplished in hand to hand, quick, well trained, and in good shape, but Max Sterling was simply unleashed lightning.

It was then that Max, blocking a punch so that he had his foe's arm in a firm lock, threw the man through the air. Only this fellow, thrashing and kicking madly, was lofted straight at Lynn-Kyle, who had been watching the fight impassively. Behind Kyle, Minmei let out a kind of squeak and ducked for cover.

Kyle never even moved his feet; he simply bent aside and struck, sending the unfortunate man flying through the air again, away from his cousin and himself.

The vigilante crashed into the table the muscular fellow had overturned, shattering it on impact as a result of the amazing force Lynn-Kyle's move had imparted to him and somehow contriving to land on his face.

Two of the brawler's friends were at his side instantly. "You all right?" one of them asked idiotically when it was obvious the man was not all right.

The brawler looked up woozily. "Who *is* that guy? He's an incredible fighter!"

"His name's Kyle," said the other buddy, "and that was nothin' but luck!" He straightened. "But I'm gonna fix him."

CHAPTER

FIFTEEN

"I'll tell ya somethin' about your Lynn-Kyle," Max said. "He might be anti-military, but he's no pacifist. What'd ya think, Gandhi could do spin kicks?"

The Collected Journals of Admiral Rick Hunter

KYLE WAITED, SERENE AND UNMOVING.

"No! *No!*" Lisa breathed, seeing them close in on him. It would be too much like having gentle Karl Riber beaten up. But there was nothing she could do; it was all she and the Terrible Trio could do to hold their own against the peripheral crowd members.

Rick wondered later if Max Sterling knew all along —or had at least guessed—what was to happen next and had deliberately thrown that first opponent Kyle's way. Max, in his supremely humble way, assured Rick that such a thing was preposterous. Rick might have believed him more if he hadn't seen the things Max could do in combat.

The first two were a pair of stumblebums; barely moving at all, Kyle disposed of them contemptuously with foot sweeps, evasions, leg trips, and beginner's-class shoulder throws.

That drew the attention of the men waiting for another crack at Max and Rick; more and more of them came at Kyle.

Minmei's cousin seemed to have chosen a particular spot on the floor and decided to defend it—not from preference but rather as an exercise of will and proficiency. Certainly, the fight didn't seem like much of a challenge—at least at first.

There was a lot of *aikido* in his style, plus *bando*, some *judo*, *uichi-ryu*, and a lot of stuff Rick couldn't identify. It wasn't until he was pressed very hard that Kyle used his feet, and after that there were teeth and blood on his area of the White Dragon's floor.

Defending himself on several fronts, Kyle didn't seem to notice the roughhouser closing in behind him. Lisa happened to see it, and she had the weird impression that he knew what was coming and chose to undergo it as a sort of test, as if he *wanted* to be hurt.

Be that as it may, the big bruiser got Kyle in a full nelson, and somebody else tagged him good and hard on the mouth. Kyle didn't seem to feel it much; he shrugged down out of the hold with some fluid move, sidekicking the man who'd done the punching so that he went down and stayed down.

Then Kyle whirled and brought the flat of his hand in an unsweeping blow along the face of the one who'd held him. The man reeled back, face leaking crimson but not as badly hurt as he would have been if Lynn-Kyle had been truly angry.

Kyle had taken just enough of the pressure off Rick and Max so that they were doing okay again. They'd both taken more than a few shots and at one time or another had, between them, squared off with just about everybody on the other side of what had become a minor war. The opponents were bouncing back more slowly now, and many of them were out of it for good.

As for Lynn-Kyle, he was a whirlwind, leaping over and ducking under, spin kicking but never surrendering the spot he'd chosen to defend in the middle of the White Dragon. He jumped impossibly high, out of the way of a powerful kick, got his opponent in a wristlock, and rammed him headfirst into a man who was attacking from the opposite side.

It was an amazing demonstration, like some martial-arts fantasy, marking the beginning of Lynn-Kyle's legend on the SDF-1. But it should be remembered that for the most part he was facing antagonists who'd already been around the dance floor once or even twice—and in some more insistent cases three times—with Rick and Max.

At one point, Rick put away a shaven-headed tough who'd been trying to gouge his eyes, working fast, jabbing combinations with knuckles that were long since lacerated and bleeding. He turned and saw Kyle, leaping high, lash out with the sword edge of his left foot and down another opponent.

Rick wiped blood from his face. "Hey, Kyle! Why don'tcha hand him a *pamphlet*?"

Rick went back to his own fight. Kyle made no response but wondered if the VT pilot knew how deeply that jape—and the dissonance of this violence—upset Kyle's inner harmonies.

The fight didn't so much end as slow to a halt; at last there was no one to come at them again. Rick was left sitting on the floor, huffing and puffing, bone-weary and sore all over. Max was panting, too, leaning against a wall, blood seeping from a swollen, split lip, his ribs starting to ache where somebody's knee had gotten a piece of him.

Lisa and the Terrible Trio were standing by the line of brawlers they'd taken out of the action, having neatly composed some of them as if for sleep. Lynn-Kyle stood squarely on the spot he'd chosen to defend in the middle of his family's restaurant.

"You okay, Rick?" Max panted.

Rick was too tired to do anything but nod slowly, tonguing a tooth that felt like it had been loosened. He felt a certain dread: There were some inflexible laws aboard the SDF-1, mandated by the insanely unlikely circumstances of so many civilians and service people thrown together in such close quarters for such a long time.

Many of those laws had to do with *"No Fighting with the Townies!"* Rick figured Gloval was going to be mildly crazy about all of this. Then it occurred to Lieutenant Hunter to think about the bigger picture, about what was happening all over the super dimensional fortress in the wake of the Boogieman's announcement.

We'll be lucky if there is an SDF-1 by tonight! he realized.

Lisa and the Terrible Trio were dusting their hands off, making a few first-aid suggestions to the people they'd taken out of the action. It occurred to Rick that without them, he and Max and even Kyle would have gone down, martial arts notwithstanding. Minmei was gazing at Kyle with stars and hearts and flowers in her eyes.

"Oh, Kyle, I'm so proud of you! Are you okay?" She threw her arms around his neck.

Lynn-Kyle only nodded and made a soft, "Mm hmm."

"'Okay'?" Rick sniggered tiredly, and spit out a gobbet of blood.

Max had come upright, staring at Kyle strangely. "They barely laid a hand on you." Kyle only looked down at the floor like some demure maiden.

Men who had been in the fight were helping each other to their feet, staunching blood flows, helping hobbling friends. One tucked an injured hand into his shirtfront with much pain, wiped the blood from his broken nose, and said grudgingly, "He's the best I've seen or fought against. That's the truth."

"Yeah," said Max Sterling reflectively. "He's got

moves *I* never saw before. Doesn't make sense." He went over toward Kyle, and Rick hauled his aching body to its feet, prepared to back up his friend if the ultimate slugfest were to begin.

There was a sudden, particular something in Max's manner now: an acuity, an unveiled dangerousness, that the aw-shucks everyday Sterling demeanor usually shrouded.

But Max only stood looking at Kyle, and Kyle back at Max. Max said after a moment, "You're a pretty well-trained fighter for someone who doesn't like to fight."

They stood measuring each other. On the one hand was quiet, bespectacled Max, with his natural gifts, miraculous coordination, and speed so superior that he could afford to be humble in all things—already a Robotech legend. Unassuming and kind unless some evil threatened. Max the placid and benign, truer to what Kyle aspired to be, in a way, than Kyle himself.

On the other hand was Kyle, seemingly apart from any worldly consideration or motivation, his incredible martial-arts skills just a reflection of things that relentlessly drove him for spiritual transcendence. People sought him, virtually courted him, sensing that he'd passed beyond everything that was superficial, and wanting—what? His attention and approval? His friendship? He didn't have them to give.

But people wanted it more than anything. Kyle's gift was a kind of cold invulnerability that brought him close to being superhuman for the most dire and yet formidable reasons, reasons that combined the very best and the very worst in him.

Those who knew certain spiritual and fighting systems could see the symptoms in him: all things lay within his grasp, excepting only that which he wanted most. So his innermost passions had been brought under control by an act of will, the dark side of his nature subdued in a battle that made lesser contests, mere physical duels, seem childishly easy.

And that made for a powerful fighter who was without fear and who would give obeisance to the very best conventional values—while his inner being fought an endless war.

Some of the people who were in the White Dragon that day later swore that the very air between Max and Kyle crackled like a kind of summer lightning or perhaps the terrifying glow between two segments of a critical mass being brought too close together.

But Kyle lowered his eyes to the floor and said softly, "It was just something that had to be done, I guess." His head came up, and he looked about at the men he'd bested. "I'm sorry." A trickle of blood ran from the corner of his mouth down to his chin.

Minmei was deciding how best to show her concern for Kyle, when Lisa stepped up to him, holding a scented, daintily folded little handkerchief in her hand. This was the woman who'd kept a rioter from pouncing on Kyle two minutes earlier by bringing down a chair on his head.

"You're bleeding! Maybe this'll help."

He drew away from it as if it carried plague, but his voice was still soft and measured. "Please don't bother. I'd rather not have help from any of you people. But thank you, anyway."

She was shattered. "I see."

Minmei was quick to see her opening and use it, snatching the handkerchief from Lisa's upturned palm. "That's right; Kyle dislikes servicemen."

Lisa stared at the floor and hoped the hot red flush of anger in her cheeks didn't show too much. Service*men*?

"Let *me* help," Minmei said, dabbing at the wound on his cheek.

Kyle hissed in pain. "It hurts if you press too hard."

She drew a quick breath. "Oh, Kyle, please forgive me!"

Punches and kicks hadn't seemed to bother him that much. "Is he for real or am I crazy?" Max muttered.

Rick shrugged; if he hadn't just seen Kyle take care of some of the more hard-core rowdies aboard the SDF-1, he would have said Minmei's cousin was a complete wimp.

If it was an act, it was brilliant. The bridge bunnies were oozing sympathy for Kyle, and somebody was going to have to stick a stretcher under Commander Hayes if she got any more emotional over his well-being, while Minmei glared at all the other women jealously and shielded Kyle from them as much as she could. Miss Macross stroked her cousin's arm with a proprietary air.

Rick turned to Max, feeling the swelling on his own forehead and the throbbing of assorted contusions suffered in the riot. "Max, if you're asking me, the answer is *yes!*" Rick told him.

Azonia, mistress and overlord of the Zentraedi, surveyed the strategic situation from the command post of her nine-mile-long flagship.

Matters were coming to a head. She was determined that *this* would be the proof of her abilities. A stellar chance! Once she defeated these Micronian upstarts, the universe would be hers. Supreme commander? That would lie well within her grasp, and farewell, Dolza!

Or perhaps she would become the *new* Robotech Mistress. Others had played that dangerous game, only to lose. But none played it as well as she, Azonia was confident.

She was less than happy at the moment, however, having just been informed that Khyron, the mad genius of war, had again disobeyed her orders.

Azonia rose to her feet from the thronelike command chair on the bridge of her own vaunted, combat-tested battleship, fury striking from her like lightning as though she were a goddess who could smash worlds.

And, in fact, Azonia was.

"What? Are you saying Khyron left the fleet's holding formation in violation of *my orders?*"

The communications officer knew that tone of voice and was quick to genuflect before her, then touch her forehead in abasement. "Yes, Commander."

She was tall even for a Zentraedi woman, some fifty-five feet and more. Her mannishly short hair had been dyed blue, not because she cared for meaningless fads but rather so she would not be thought *unaware*.

She had exotic, oblique eyes that were piercing beam weapons of intellect that had served Azonia's rise beyond her contemporaries to the very pinnacle of Zentraedi command. "That is all," she said coldly.

"Yes, Commander." The messenger withdrew quickly and very gratefully; beheading the bearer of bad news was a not-uncommon Zentraedi custom, which among other things served to keep the lower orders in their place. She was glad—and lucky—to have her life.

But Azonia had dismissed the messenger from her mind completely; her concentration was all for the problem at hand. Technical readouts and displays told her all the details she needed to know: The Backstabber, with a strike force from his infamous Seventh Mechanized Division had, by Robotech fission, detached a major vessel-form from his own flagship and was proceeding at flank speed toward the spot where the Micronians had landed their stolen starship.

Azonia touched a control almost languidly. Close-up details showed streamers of fire and ionization trailing from Khyron's craft, its outermost skin glowing red-hot; he was making his entry into the Earth's atmosphere at a madly acute angle, risking severe friction damage.

Azonia had sufficient experience to know that Khyron and his attack troops were sitting out a roller coaster ride in an oven, all in the name of a possible extra few minutes of surprise.

It was so audacious. It was so willful, so disdainful of anyone's criticism or interference. So Zentraedi. Azonia resumed her throne, chin on fist. "Khyron, what have you come up with this time, eh?"

She was in some small part envious, sorry that she wouldn't be there for the fight. With Khyron in charge, there was sure to be a splendid battle, bloodshed—that highest glory that was *conquest*.

On a previous venture, Khyron had been yanked from his objective at the last moment by Breetai's manual-override return command, which had caused the Backstabber's war machines to return to the fleet despite his countermanding orders. Khyron had apparently taken steps to ensure that it couldn't happen to him again.

By now the Earthlings would be hearing the peal of Khyron's thunder. Azonia, eyes slitted like a cat's, savored the moment, knowing she couldn't lose either way. If the Backstabber won, the credit would go to her as armada commander, she would make sure of that; if he lost and was unfortunate or unwise enough to return to the fleet, she would have the pleasure of executing him herself.

Azonia savored the thought. Violence and death and a certain sensual cruelty were things to command any Zentraedi's emotions. Khyron was becoming quite intriguing.

Azonia watched the displays with feline glee. Decorate him, kill him; she was equally eager to do either one.

CHAPTER
SIXTEEN

There before him were the Micronians, doing everything that was anathema to the Zentraedi. But the lure of the forbidden was always strong in Khyron, and so there were certain things about Micronian behavior that, I think, he found tremendously seductive—not the weakling things, of course, but rather the sensual.

Is it any wonder he loathed and hated them, could not bear to have them even exist?

Grel, aide to Khyron

SHE'D BEEN THROUGH THIS DRILL BEFORE, BUT IT didn't make it any easier. Donna Wilhelm, an enlisted-rating tech who was relief-watch fill-in for Sammie, tried not to lose her composure and let her voice quaver.

Her fingers clenched at the edges of the console, so hard that it felt like she might crease it. "Captain Gloval, unidentified cruiser-class spacecraft closing on our position at Mach seven."

She was the one Claudia had chewed out for daydreaming; Donna was exacting now, more practiced. She'd learned the lessons anybody under Gloval learned, and as a result she was capable of manning her station through hell's own flames. Which looked like it was about to become a job requirement.

Donna hadn't heard footsteps, but Gloval was suddenly at her shoulder, massive and calm, whacking his briar pipe against the heel of his shoe to knock out a bit of dottle. "Punch it up, please."

"Yes, sir. Altitude twelve thousand." Donna lit up her part of the bridge with tactical displays. It was a given that this could be the minute in which every soul aboard died.

But that couldn't excuse sloppiness in the discharge of one's obligations. There was a pure, white-hot kind of *bushido*, an ultimate calmness in matters of overwhelming importance, a very privileged eye-of-the-storm serenity, that the people on the bridge of SDF-1 were expected to have.

Once you'd been a part of it, it was just impossible to settle for anything less. Donna had learned it in a school that permitted very few errors and *no* inattention, under Gloval, Lisa Hayes, Claudia Grant, and the others.

So now Donna did her duty, up to SDF-1 standards, which is to say without flaw and with the guts of a cat burglar. "Eleven thousand," she updated. "If it maintains present course, it'll touch down approx ten miles from the SDF-1 magnetic bearing three-two-five."

It couldn't be anything but trouble; the war was on again, and if peace had seemed too good to be true, that was because it *was*. But Gloval's broad hand patted Donna's shoulder for a moment, transferring what felt like an infinite calm even while he was calling orders to other bridge personnel.

"Order up a B status encrypted comline to headquarters immediately! And one of you find Commander Hayes and get her up here on the double! Somebody else tell Ghost and Skull teams to get ready for a hot scramble!"

People were doing all of that, and still the bridge was as quiet as a well-run switchboard. Gloval told Donna Wilhelm, "Well done. Give me updates every fifteen seconds, understood? And if you see I'm not listening, come stand on my foot."

Then he was gone, and the SDF-1 bridge was quietly

chaotic with a general-quarters combat alert. Arm Hammerhead missiles and Deca missiles and Scorpion missiles; power up to main gun batteries; secondaries; to all firing positions. Hot scrambles, ready on go, aye.

Donna looked at her screens and got ready to relay the first update to Gloval. Over a year ago, her family had been one of those that were simply vacuumed up in the catastrophic first encounter between Zentraedi and human. Now her father was an emergency team specialist, her mother supervised an elite EVA squad, and her younger brother was dead, one of Ghost Team's KIAs back in that big blitzkrieg in Saturn's rings.

So Donna did her duty. The aliens had followed SDF-1 to Earth; the aliens would follow the SDF-1 everywhere, hound the ship and hound those within it until this fight was settled one way or the other. Only, there was one thing that the aliens didn't seem to understand: The SDF-1's crew would never surrender now.

No matter; it was war again. And the Zentraedi didn't know that they themselves were refining, like precious metals in some torturous crucible, a counterforce within the human race that was their match—in willpower if not in firepower—and more.

Much more.

In the vast command center under the Alaskan wilderness, an operator called out over his headset, "Confirmed enemy craft continues descent, sir. Will touch down at point K-32, R-56 Bravo."

The duty officer, Brigadier General Theroux, leaned forward, staring up at the immense display screen. "Are you certain? Are you positive that that craft is confirmed as the enemy?"

"That's affirmative, sir."

Theroux got to his feet, squaring away his cap. This was Command's worst fear made real. The Grand Cannon wasn't yet ready to fire, and even if it had been, the approaching alien warship wasn't in its range. Until the planned network of unique dish satellites was in place to redirect the Grand Cannon's superbolts as needed, it was virtually useless.

Theroux opened an emergency com channel, sure that the ruling council would want to reconsider standing instructions under the circumstances. But he could reach only General Herbert and Marshal Zukav.

"And the enemy is headed straight for the SDF-1," Theroux finished his brief situation report.

General Herbert's face blinked at him out of the screen. "And? You mean you haven't carried out Special Order Seventy-three yet?"

Theroux said desperately, "But sir, that will only—"

"Carry out your duty!" Zukav screamed, florid-faced, from another screen. "Do it this instant or I'll personally see you hanged for mutiny!" The screens blanked.

That will only goad them into attacking the SDF-1, and the SDF-1 is a sitting duck, Theroux had been about to say. But Herbert and Zukav knew that as well as he. It was as if they *wanted* the battle fortress obliterated—

Brigadier General Theroux forced his thoughts away from that line of contemplation. He had his orders.

He addressed his launch control officer. "Very well, then: execute Special Order Seventy-three. Launch missiles immediately."

And as techs were acknowledging and carrying out the command, he murmured, "And heaven help us."

"We are now monitoring all base com signals and telemetry," Claudia reported.

"Very good," Gloval said. While he had no direct orders *not* to eavesdrop on his superiors, it went against all operating procedure. But he had so few things working to his advantage in this crisis; if a man with cloven hooves, smelling of brimstone, had appeared on the bridge at that moment, it's very likely that the captain would have struck a bargain with him.

Claudia looked over to Lisa, who seemed lost in

thought even though her boards appeared to be registering a lot of activity. "Lisa?" Claudia called softly. "Lisa! Girl, what seems to be the problem? You've been in some kind of daydream ever since you got back. Tell me, is it Kyle?"

For a moment Lisa looked like a startled deer. Then she became very defensive, even though she should have been used to her best friend's teasing by then. "Claudia, you know that's just not true!"

"Ahem," Gloval said softly, materializing behind them. "Ladies . . ."

They both got back to work, but Claudia was chuckling and an angry red spot appeared on each of Lisa's cheeks.

Kim shattered the gentle, joking atmosphere for good. "Captain, headquarters had just launched defense missiles. Our instruments show approximately fifteen seconds to impact."

Gloval settled into his chair. "Fifteen seconds, understood." *What in blazes can those fools be hoping to accomplish? Conventional weapons are totally useless against the Zentraedi.*

"Prepare to send in the Veritechs," he said.

With the disappearance of Dr. Lang and the SDF-1 and the destruction of its orbital force in the wake of the initial Zentraedi attack, Earth's defense command had been forced to fall back on older technologies, at least until their Grand Cannon was completed.

Even the production of VTs was impossible, since most of the necessary fabricating and power-plant replicating devices were on the battle fortress; the earthly RDF fighters who'd greeted the ship on its return were just that, ordinary fighters, even though they *looked* like VTs. The only real Robotech weapons now in the Council's possession were the handful of Battloids that had, predictably, been preempted to guard the Council's own Alaskan warren.

The huge, silvery missiles that rose up from the planet's surface now, recently manufactured and bearing the kite-like delta insignia of the Robotech Defense Forces, were nevertheless primitive in comparison with Robotechnology. But the order to fire was in place, and the workings of command structure spun and reacted automatically.

Khyron's great cruiser moved more slowly in the thick lower atmosphere. He didn't even bother trying to evade the missiles or shoot them down; he relished the shudder and thunder of their harmless detonations against his vessel's massive armor. He loved toying with his prey, loved to pretend that slaughter was battle.

Hellish fire washed across the ship's armor and swirled away behind it, like foam off a killer whale, having no effect.

Behind the big transparent bubble of his command post, Khyron looked down contentedly at the activity on his warship's bridge. Grel, his second in command, growled in a fierce, deep Zentraedi guttural, "Khyron, what about a counterattack?"

It was Khyron's pleasure to speak differently from his fellows, to be unique in all things. His accent was over-refined, almost foppish, though the Zentraedi lacked such a concept except in his case. But few people had ever dared call the Backstabber on it, and all of those had met with grief.

"A brilliant idea, Grel! But just what are we counterattacking?"

Grel's thick brows met as he pondered the question. "You mean," he said slowly, "that this planet is not the actual main objective."

Khyron's handsome, sinister face lit with a predatory smile. "You're beginning to see the light." Another glorious victory for Khyron! And oblivion for the hated SDF-1; things were going perfectly.

* * *

"Veritechs, you have permission to engage the enemy," Lisa said. "Fire at will."

A swarm of angry VTs swooped in on the descending alien, lances of bright blue energy stabbing from their pulsed laser-array cannon, another of Lang's developments.

"SDF-1 to United Earth Command," Lisa transmitted. "Our fighter squadron has initiated contact." *Chew on* that, *you burrowing moles!*

The VTs were in close, flown by veterans who knew where to aim and how to avoid the bigger ship's clumsy cannon volleys. They did only minor damage on the first few passes; but there were dozens of them, so more serious damage would be inflicted if they were allowed to have their way.

Gloval was counting on something he'd noticed before: There were definitely differing factions among the enemy, sometimes working at cross-purposes. One faction seemed to be commanded by an injudicious hothead, and this attack smacked of him—or her.

Gloval was right. Even as the enemy cruiser closed on the dimensional fortress, fighter bays opened and alien mecha poured forth to battle for the skies. For this engagement, Khyron had elected to use a mix of his best fighting machines; the VTs swooped in to find themselves facing stubby triple-engine fighters with fuselages like narrow eggs: tri-thrusters—Botoru pursuit ships, agile and spoiling for a fight.

But no more so than the RDF fliers, who were now on their home planet, their backs literally to the sea. There was nowhere to run, no thought of surrender, and no battle plan needed except to make the aliens pay very, very dearly for each moment they spent in Earth's atmosphere.

"I'm getting heavy contact reports and increased readings of enemy activity, sir," Claudia relayed.

Out where war mecha jousted with spears of pure ruin

for the fate of the SDF-1 and the human race, lines of fire
and counterfire crisscrossed ferociously, taking a heavy
toll on both sides.

Despite a steady rain of blasts from the SDF-1's primary and secondary batteries, Khyron's cruiser swung
in a low pass toward the battle fortress. Gloval wasted
no time wishing that the all-powerful main gun could be
fired. That wasn't possible; damage to the main gun
mechanism suffered on reentry hadn't been repaired yet.
So the battle would have to be won another way.

More VTs were ordered to the flight decks, Rick's
Vermilions among them, and every weapon on the ship
concentrated fire on the invader. Gloval spoke quickly to
engineering, preparing for other, desperate measures.

The SDF-1's fire was punishing Khyron's ship as even
the VTs couldn't, but that didn't matter to the Backstabber; he needed only a little longer. His cruiser passed
overhead, all batteries firing, the two heavyweight ships
hammering away at each other with all they had, inflicting appalling damage.

At the same time the cruiser released more mecha, a
virtual hail of Battlepods that dropped down toward the
SDF-1. The pods and the tri-thruster pursuit ships kept
up a heavy fusillade. The VTs did their best to turn back
the assault drop, but they were simply outnumbered;
there would be many empty bunks down in the squadron
quarters that night, if indeed the SDF-1 lasted at all.

Leading his troops in his own tremendously powerful
officer's Battlepod, Khyron saw the carnage and grinned
like a lunatic.

"Keep firing and don't stop until we've destroyed
every last one of the miserable Micronian vermin!"

CHAPTER
SEVENTEEN

And so the stage was set by the eternal mandala, the yin and the yang—the good that is in evil, and the evil that is in good. Human betrayal, Zentraedi disobedience of several kinds, and yes, that fanatic courage of the aliens—these all played their part that day.

Jan Morris,
Solar Seeds, Galactic Guardians

CLAUDIA TURNED TO CALL TO GLOVAL. "A MIXED group of fighting vehicles is approaching our decks, sir. The Veritechs couldn't hold them."

"I want Vermilion ready for immediate launch," Gloval snapped.

Lisa found herself seeing Rick's face and shook her head to regain her concentration. "Yes, sir."

As his ship and Max Sterling's were raised to the flight deck, Rick thought, *Well, here we go again. And how many will die this time? Damn all Zentraedi! You want death?*

Come on, then; we'll give you death!

Claudia updated, "Enemy breakthrough heaviest now at blocks three, seven, niner, and sixteen."

146

Gloval turned and called, "Get the tactical corps mecha out on deck. Double-check to make sure all civil defense mecha are in position and have them stand by for possible redeployment!"

Everybody knew what that meant: Gloval was practically admitting that the aliens might penetrate to the very interior of the ship itself—perhaps to Macross City.

Lisa shuddered, but she kept on at her work, seemingly calm and self-possessed. "Vermilion Team, stand by at block number three for protection and await further orders." From that position a number of the dimensional fortress's functioning gun turrets and missile tubes could provide some cover for them until Gloval decided where to commit them.

"Roger," Rick acknowledged.

Almost all the other VT teams were either in the air or waiting to be lifted to the flight deck, but that didn't seem to be daunting the enemy. More and more alien mecha were dropping, an unbelievable assault force. *That cruiser must have been packed cheek by jowl with them!* Lisa thought.

She saw Vermilion forming up on an outboard pickup. Enemy fire was sizzling down all around them, blue-white beams that vaporized the nonskid and scored the armor deeply.

Rick's voice came on again. "Hey there, Commander Hayes! How many of these things do we have to shoot down before they stop coming at us? Ten thousand or twenty thousand? Or two million, or what? Just checking, you understand."

A sudden volley hit right near his VT and almost got it; she could hear the shock and adrenaline in his voice as he cried out, "God damn you!" at the aliens.

Lisa looked stunned. "Hold position," she said slowly, feeling her skin go cold and her heart pounding so hard she could feel it all through her. She watched her screen, hypnotized, waiting for the next salvo to claim him.

"Await . . . further orders . . ." she managed. She saw

Rick's face before her, in a cockpit, but then suddenly Karl Riber's—or no, it was Lynn-Kyle's, wasn't it? What was happening to her?

There was such a thing as personal initiative, and junior officers—especially team leaders—were expected to recognize a time when it was their duty to exercise it.

"Well, I'm getting these fighters out of here before it's too late!" Rick snapped, as much to himself as to Commander Hayes. "All right, Vermilion; follow me!"

There was no time for a catapult launch, even if the cat crews had been able to function in that firestorm. None could, and many of the brave crews were down for good.

The VTs rolled behind Rick, engines shrilling; only Robotechnology gave them power to reach sufficient airspeed in the short space available. Rick's VT howled out into the air, followed by Max, Ben, and the rest.

Even so, they hadn't gotten away fast enough. The fifth VT took a direct hit while lifting, crashed to the deck again, burning out of control because overworked damage and firefighting crews were fully occupied elsewhere. From the explosion, it was clear that the pilot had died instantly.

But the deck would have to be cleared for more launches and for eventual landings, assuming any Veritechs came back this day. A courageous cat crew officer named Moira Flynn climbed into a cargo mover. Braving the flames, the exploding VT ordnance, and the withering enemy fire, she began bulldozing the wreckage to the edge of the deck, to dump it into the sea.

Lisa could barely spare an instant in which to watch the launch of Vermilion; there were a thousand other things that demanded her attention. But she shut her eyes for an instant. *Please let him be all right!* But Rick's face was superimposed in her mind with Karl's, with Kyle's . . .

* * *

Out on the flight deck, a bulky Gladiator attack mecha from the tactical corps—a smaller, cruder version of the Battloids—fired its chest cannon, missile racks, and straight-lasers. It suddenly found itself confronted by a quintet of Battlepods that dropped to the deck almost simultaneously, blowing the Gladiator away; both human crewmembers were dead practically before they knew what was happening.

More pods landed, firing the heavy guns mounted on their plastrons and, in some special cases, missile launchers, particle cannon, and other offensive armaments.

Two more Gladiators came forward to seal the hole in the defensive lines, braving the enemy rounds to throw out a wall of fire of their own. The crewmembers loved life as much as anybody, but they were unswerving in the defense of their ship and their planet. They opened up with gatlings and missiles and lasers. The Battlepods kept coming until the mecha were at point-blank range.

Another Gladiator went down. Amid the smoke and confusion, the third found itself out of ammunition and standing toe to toe with a pod.

The Gladiator crew reacted at once; as the pod sprang at it, their war machine swung an armored fist, caving in the lower half of the Zentraedi's plastron. The Gladiator ducked, and the pod crashed to the deck a little beyond.

Unarmed, the RDF mecha turned to grapple with the next pod, but it leapt high in the air like an immense grasshopper, all guns firing. The Gladiator collapsed in on itself, becoming a fireball.

Rick lined up another bogey, one of the small, fiendishly fast Botoru pursuit ships. The enemy fired a poorly aimed stream of the annihilating energy discs that were one of its armaments, then flared like a meteor before the Vermilion Leader's volley.

The battle was the biggest fighter ratrace yet, all the

more frantic and hysterical because it swirled through the relatively small area around the battle fortress. Speeds were therefore much lower than usual, but distances were so short and maneuvering room so limited that everything happened in split seconds.

One dogfight got mixed up with another. Pilots from both sides collided, shot friend instead of foe, lost sight of their prey only to find a bandit on their tail.

Lisa's voice sounded in Rick's headphones. "Proceed to enemy penetration at block number seven."

Only Max and Ben were left now. They managed to make it over to the designated defensive block, where they were witnesses to something out of an old-time Western movie.

Civil Defense mecha had been rushed up to serve as reinforcements for the tacticals. The thickset war machines, like walking dreadnoughts, stood straddle-legged on the deck, blasting away at the massed enemy.

Excalibur Mark VIs and Gladiators, drum-armed Spartans with their huge circular canisters of missile launchers, and multibarreled Raider Xs swinging their beam cannon this way and that—they all stood shoulder to shoulder against the main Zentraedi onslaught as enemy fire took them out of the line one by one.

The pods were closing in fast; the enormous losses they'd suffered seemed to have no effect on the size of the fleet. They had advanced to a point where none of the SDF-1's primary batteries—and only a few of the remaining secondaries—had a line of fire on them; the batteries were primarily for air defense.

The RDF mecha were standing their ground, laying down fire with everything they had. They knew that if their line collapsed, there would be nothing to stop the aliens from getting into the ship—and winning the war.

It was truly the hour of the attack mecha, with even the VTs taking a back seat. They made their stand as the Zentraedi closed the distance by leaps and bounds. The killing in the skies had numbed him, yet

Rick thought this was one of the most savage scenes ever seen during the war.

As Vermilion came in to see what they could do to help, two foremost Raider Xs went up like cans of fire-crackers. The pods bounded past the wreckage to close in on the last of the defenders.

Khyron was gleeful, nearly mad with the joy of war, as he led the final charge, addressing the cannon of his Officer's Pod to a new target. In minutes, the ship would be his; and with it, the universe.

In the meantime, three of the accursed VTs made a close strafing run, destroying the leading line of pods. But other pods would soon be there to deal with them; even Veritechs couldn't keep Zor's ultimate creation away from Khyron now!

Khyron was distracted by two lumbering Excaliburs that were closing in on him, their power low, missile racks exhausted. He blew them both away in the same moment with the tremendous derringerlike cannon that were arms of the Officer's Pod.

The VTs were making another pass, and the enemy mecha were being outrageously stubborn—but the final conclusion should only take another minute or so.

But just then Khyron heard an alarm signal on his instrument panel. He read his indicators, turned, and craned to look up into the distant sky. "What's this? *No! Impossible!*"

Grimly, without looking up from her data displays, Claudia said, "Captain, a second enemy attack force is on the way down now, from another ship. They appear to be a new type of mecha."

Leading her combat drop, Miriya looked approvingly at the bitter struggle raging all around the dimensional fortress. Behind her came a full battalion of her Quadrono Battalion's powered armor mecha.

Azonia was still reiterating instructions over the com

net, a rather offensive bit of interference, Miriya thought. "Miriya, the purpose of your operation is to thwart Khyron's plan. Therefore, do not fire at the enemy or damage the dimensional fortress."

Azonia had done some thinking in the interim and had consulted several of her personal informants. It seemed Khyron was playing a game truly his own; everything pointed to his intention to take the SDF-1 for himself.

And Azonia would win no approval from her superiors or the Robotech Masters if that were to happen; quite the opposite, in fact. Thus: Miriya and her Quadrono Battalion were launched to stop him.

So a Zentraedi warrior is expected not to fire at the enemy, eh? Miriya smiled to herself maliciously. "Well now, it's too bad I never heard that order because my communications gear is malfunctioning, Azonia!"

Her own personal mecha-suit was the one that had so dazzled the RDF during her insertion of the three spies. It was supercharged, more maneuverable and powerful than any other in the Zentraedi fleet. Now she zoomed down like a lightning bolt, blowing an unsuspecting VT out of the air with a double stream of the annihilation discs, destroying another a split second later.

"I love it when a good plan works out well," she said languidly. And the good plan in this case was her own— the one that had gotten her another crack at the enemy and, if she was lucky, a little scuffle with Khyron's incompetents as well.

The Quadrono armor hit thrusters, rocketing for the deck.

Azonia ranted at the com pickup in her flagship bridge command center. "Khyron, come in immediately! Can you hear me? You are in violation of your orders! Therefore, stop this attack at once!"

Perhaps he would claim that his equipment wasn't working properly. That was the damnable thing about the Zentraedi armada, and for that matter their whole instrumentality. With a few exceptions like that bitch Miriya's, Zentraedi war machinery had a far from flawless operational record.

It was only right that warriors care only for war; maintenance and mechanics were work for slaves. But there never seemed to be nearly enough of those, at least ones of any use.

Azonia swore under her breath and waited to see what would happen.

But Khyron wasn't opposed to answering her. He was merely completing his latest maneuver, having leapt his pod high to come down directly over two of the last enemy attack mecha, a pair of Raider Xs, blowing them to bits with the derringer cannon.

"Violation of my orders?" he mocked her. "But I haven't done anything to these despicable Micronians, at least not yet!" He was firing to all sides. "But in the centuries to come, if any of them are left alive, they will speak the name of Khyron with terror!"

"Don't play games with me!" Azonia shouted. "Turn back at once or I'll have you shot!"

The last of the enemy mecha were down, and Khyron was about to lead his forces to the ultimate plunder, when the odds suddenly changed. Aircraft elevator platforms ground up into view to either side despite the fact that the last of the SDF-1 combat aircraft had long since taken off.

They were loaded, instead, with every MAC II Destroid cannon the desperate defenders had managed to get to the trouble spot, arriving in time only because of the attack mecha's courageous last stand and Vermilion's skillful flying. Six of the stumpy, waddling gun turrets were on either elevator, port and starboard.

Mounting six pulsed laser-array cannon and four supervelocity electromagnetic rail-guns apiece, the MACs had the pods in a perfect cross fire—and opened up.

What had been imminent victory for the pods became instead a disastrous firestorm.

The rail-guns fired solid slugs at a velocity that delivered incredible kinetic energy on impact, velocities so high that making the slugs explosive would have been redundant. Zentraedi combat armor was no protection, and Battlepods collapsed in on themselves like crushed eggs or came apart in fragments, only to explode instants later.

The MACs' pulsed lasers swept back and forth at the massed alien war mecha, quartering the sky with grazing fire that raked the flight deck, and caught them as they leapt or while still on their feet. Pods went up like exploding oil-well rigs or expanding spheres of shrapnel and flame.

Khyron had instantly leapt his pod away to comparative safety upon seeing the MACs appear. He would have gone truly berserk with frustration and wrath at that point, but his own life was now at stake.

There would be no quick taking of the objective, and SDF-1's deck was being swept clear of his troops. More, Miriya's hated Quadronos were hovering above, out of range but capable of intervening at any moment. But on whose side? In some ways she was as capable of duplicity as Khyron himself.

And then, of course, there was Azonia's promise to have him shot.

He gave a low, bestial growl as he landed his Battlepod on a safer area of the deck, opening his command channel. "All right, men! Cease firing! We're returning to the fleet!"

His mission exec, Gerao, came up over the net, sounding shocked. "Ex-excuse me, mighty Khyron; would you please repeat that? We're going back *now*?"

Khyron could see from his instruments that Gerao was fairly well in the clear and could reach the cruiser quickly. The cruiser was exactly where he'd directed that it be: submerged in the ocean not far from SDF-1.

"Yes." Khyron sneered. "I have just received a direct order from Commander Azonia. "But—don't forget to get your *souvenir*, my friend."

"My *souvenir*?" Gerao's tone said he'd understood Khyron's hidden meaning. "Why, no, sir. I certainly won't forget that!"

Khyron began regrouping his forces for the shameful withdrawal. But part of him burned fusion-bright.

If Khyron couldn't have his victory, he would at least have his revenge!

CHAPTER
EIGHTEEN

> *No one, gunner or VT jock or attack-mecha crew-member, could recall a more intense fight. Certainly they all earned their pay that day, and a lot more than money besides. Many paid the final price of freedom.*
>
> *It is interesting to note, however, that although everyone on the VT teams had seen intense combat, it was the men and woman of the air-sea rescue teams [whose units had also suffered heavy casualties] who, upon entering the various pilots' hangouts, found that they would not be allowed to pay for their own drinks, period.*
>
> Zachary Fox, Jr., *VT: the Men and the Mecha*

THE GIANT SAUCER SHAPES THAT WERE ZENTRAEDI amphibious-assault ships dropped from Miriya's cruiser to retrieve Khyron's surviving Battlepods.

At Khyron's order, the first of his retreating units kangaroo-hopped from the SDF-1's deck into the sea to get well clear of the fortress's guns and fighters before making their rendezvous. He'd lost enough of his vaunted strike force without having them and their pickup ships shot out of the sky.

Now it was Zentraedi mecha that fought the holding action as RDF attack machines and VTs pressed them ever harder and turned the kill ratios around. Battlepods bobbed and churned through the waves as the great saucers descended for the rendezvous point.

Overhead, the fighters were still going at it with the Botoru tri-thruster pursuit ships while the SDF-1's gun batteries took more and more enemy ships out of the fight as the tactical and civil defense attack mecha took over mop-up operations on deck.

Elsewhere, Gerao reached Khyron's cruiser as it rose from its submerged position. He gave quick orders as his pod was being brought aboard, preparing to take command and wreak Khyron's vengeance on the Micronians.

Vanessa called out, "Captain, that first enemy cruiser has reappeared! It's on a collision course with us!"

Gloval thumbed the bowl of his empty pipe absentmindedly. "It looks like a suicide maneuver. Lisa, Claudia! Prepare the *Daedalus* for its Attack mode, immediately!"

Up on deck, Vermilion Team had its Veritechs in Battloid mode.

Rick concentrated on control, letting his helmet's receptors pick up his thought-commands and translate them into the Battloid's instant, fluid movements. The Battloid traversed its autocannon from one target to the next, firing depleted transuranic slugs that had awesome, armor-piercing capabilities. The powered gatling consumed ammunition at an amazing rate, and the Battloid had to transfer fresh boxed belts of rounds to it frequently from integral reserve modules built into various parts of its body.

The reloading took only moments, but in the middle of a firefight that could be a long time. Rick found himself on empty as a pod dashed at him. He hit the thrusters built into the Battloid's feet and launched himself at it, just as its cannonade blew up the deck where he'd been standing.

He had no choice but to attack it hand to hand before it could get a bead on him. All around him, Battloids were locked in similar close-quarters fighting against the pods, up and down the SDF-1's decks.

But the alien Battlepod crewman was shrewd and

quick. The pod lashed out with one foot and sent Rick's Battloid flying backward with a tooth-rattling jolt. The Battloid crashed to the deck, its pilot dazed.

He shook his head clear just in time to send the Battloid rolling to the side. He avoided the pod's next fusillade, rolled again, and brought the Battloid to its feet dexterously. And now, the chain-gun was reloaded.

Rick fired a long burst, taking the pod dead center; he watched it dissolve and fly into pieces, an expanding, blazing sphere. But out of the ballooning explosion zoomed a new enemy, one of those strange alien mecha that had been mostly staying out of the fight up until now.

Whoever was flying it was either a masterful pilot or crazy or both. The battle-armored figure came through the fireball in one piece, though, and nearly bowled Rick over. Its weapons came close to downing Max on one side and Ben on the other as the two Vermilion wingmen dove for cover.

The lightning-fast attacker was gone before they could fire at it, since the SDF-1's surviving batteries were hopelessly slow in tracking it. The three Vermilion fliers got their Battloids to their feet, shaken but unharmed.

"Let's finish this thing!" Rick said in clipped tones. At his command, Vermilion went into Veritech mode, skimming the deck, turning pods into expanding balls of incandescent gas with intense autocannon fire.

The last few pods leapt high, thrusters cutting in, trying for a slim-chance vertical escape while the remaining Botoru pursuit ships dove to try to cover them. The lower battle and the upper became one as the mecha swirled and fought. Rick peeled off to go after two escaping pods.

"So they think they have won, eh?" Khyron mused, his pod standing in the shelter of a superstructural feature of the dimensional fortress's flight deck, hidden and waiting.

*   *   *

Rick bagged the pods, and Ben and Max went back down to take care of an insistent pursuit ship that was still strafing the SDF-1. They returned to Battloid mode, blasting it into ten thousand pieces.

Meanwhile, Rick had picked up two more tri-thrusters on his tail. He led them down to deck level, and Max and Ben bagged them from behind with streams of high-density slugs.

"Nice shooting!" Rick said, relieved. Then he saw what was coming up fast behind him. "No!"

It was the strange alien attack mecha, the one that had nearly nailed him moments before. He braced himself to be hit, perhaps killed, then and there. But it zoomed past, gaining altitude rapidly, pulling away as if the VT were standing still.

Rick realized that it matched the description of that souped-up Zentraedi who had done so much damage to Roy Fokker's Skull Team just before the Skulls recovered the stolen pod in which Lisa, Rick, Ben, and Max had made their escape from the aliens.

Rick cut in auxiliary power, going ballistic, determined to end the warped cat-and-mouse game.

In her special suit of Quadrono powered armor, Miriya laughed scornfully.

Khyron's cruiser was close enough to the SDF-1 that the ship's turret guns were making serious hits on it now. The remaining Battloids on the deck were also keeping up a steady volume of fire at the suicide ship. But that was of no matter; in moments, the battle would be over.

In his massively reinforced command center, Gerao braced for collision.

"Veritechs, be ready to get clear on my command," Claudia said, having taken over some direction of fighter ops while Lisa readied the *Daedalus* Maneuver.

Miriya swept by, only a few feet off the deck. Rick

was right on her tail, chasing her high and low, around and around.

She went into another climb, but the irritating Micronian stayed with her in the six o'clock position, chopping away at her with autocannon fire.

Not that it concerned her very much; Miriya was sure she could turn on him and kill hilm whenever she chose. But she monitored the coming impact of the enormous ships closely. "Khyron, do not fail!"

"*Daedalus* attack in five seconds," Claudia marked. "Four..."

The Terrible Trio braced for collision; the enemy cruiser blocked the sky, growing larger every instant.

In one horrifying moment, Claudia realized that Lisa was paralyzed.

Lisa saw Rick's face, saw poor dead Karl's, saw Kyle's. Over and over, so obsessively that she failed to see the cruiser's bow filling the bridge's forward viewbowl.

"*LISA!*"

Claudia's shout brought her back at the very last moment. Her hands were reacting even before she could order her thoughts, flying across the controls. She heard herself responding calmly, "Executing *Daedalus* attack now." It was as if someone else were speaking.

They felt the SDF-1 shift, its bouyancy radically altered, as the supercarrier *Daedalus* was lifted clear of the water—a battering ram the size of a hundred-fifty story building. There was the rumble of the dimensional fortress's foot thrusters firing to keep balance. The sea boiled all around them.

The astoundingly powerful Robotech servos lifted the huge flatdeck clear of the sea, thrusting it at the incoming enemy like a titanic warrior throwing a slow-motion punch.

Gerao saw the carrier's prow coming; it was far too late to do anything about it. He triggered his personal ejection mechanism, to flee the ship while he still could, leaving the rest of his crew to perish.

The *Daedalus*'s hurricane bow and can-opener prow had been reinforced by Lang and his technicians to the point where they were all but invulnerable, even against Zentraedi armor. *Daedalus* punched through the cruiser's hull, keelside and forward, as if skewering it. The carrier burst through armor, structural members, bulkheads, and systemry, smashing everything that was in its path as if it were passing through rotted wood and plasterboard.

The cruiser's velocity carried it into the blow, and the SDF-1's incomparable power lifted *Daedalus* and the enemy vessel high. The supercarrier's prow emerged from the cruiser's upper side, protruding more than fifty yards beyond.

Lisa, still monitoring the attack and shaken by her near failure, hadn't noticed that protrusion. She was alarmed that the cruiser's residual momentum was grinding it forward toward the SDF-1 like a wild boar coming up a hunter's spear to deal death before it died.

"Emergency missiles: Fire!" she said, hitting the switch.

High above, the carrier's bow swung open and a thousand missiles screamed out of their launchers. But instead of seeking targets within the enemy vessel, as they were programmed to do and as they had done in the the Battle at Saturn's Rings, they boiled out into the open sky.

Here and there they found a damaged, limping Battlepod or a disabled Botoru tri-thruster, obliterating them; but the majority climbed, searching for targets and rose up at—a Veritech.

He juked and hit his countermeasures and jamming gear, giving his ship everything he had while simultaneously screaming over the command net.

"Lisa, this is Rick! I'm in direct line of our missiles! Abort firing! Destruct! Destroy them!"

She'd barely begun when he was yelling, "Mayday! Mayday, I'm hit!"

The jolt to his wing and another to the rear stabilizers, as well as the sudden, uncontrollable spin, let him know that there was no hope of keeping his VT in the air. He was preparing to eject when another missile hit the fuselage forward of the wing—just below the cockpit.

Above the VT that pursued her and slightly farther away from the missile barrage, Azonia gave her powered armor suit maximum emergency power, dodging and diving. The explosions of the missiles that had hit Rick's ship had set off fratricide explosions in other missiles, causing them to destroy one another and upsetting the guidance systems of many more.

She turned, dove, shook off the last of the missiles chasing her, and came back past the SDF-1 in a low pass that clipped the tops off the ocean swells heated by the dimensional fortress's thrusters. Her jamming equipment, the surface clutter, and her own speed and maneuverability had somehow saved her. Unscathed, she flashed into the sky once more as the missile barrage died away.

Khyron's cruiser was beginning to glow and tremble from massive interior damage and ruptured power systems. Claudia and the others moved fast to pull the *Daedalus* free and back away. They were barely clear when the cruiser's engines overloaded and it became a globe of blinding light, rocking the SDF-1 in the water.

"The follow-up missile attack on the enemy was a complete success!" Claudia crowed. "Captain, the enemy ship has been totally destroyed!"

Looking down from his hovering Battlepod, far out of the radius of battle, missile attack, and explosion, Khyron pounded his metalshod fist against the arm of his seat over and over.

"No! My plans can't have failed! Not again! I won't have it!"

Azonia's image appeared on one of his screens. "Well, Khyron, it looks as though your perfect plan was slightly less than perfect. In fact, if it had been any *less* perfect, you'd be dead too!" Her jeering laugh let him know that such an event wouldn't have been so imperfect to her.

The remaining enemy forces withdrew in their big saucer-like amphibious ships. Gloval vetoed any idea of pursuit. "Let's not push our luck *or* theirs, eh? The battle is over." He rose to go. "Just maintain present position."

"Yes, Captain," Claudia responded, when Lisa didn't.

He paused to look back at Lisa. "Oh, and Commander Hayes: I want to commend you on the excellent job you did this afternoon."

They all saw her shoulders shaking as she bent over her console, heard the sobs in her voice as she replied, "Thank you, sir."

Later, as she sat in her cabin, her head whirled with bits and pieces of the things that were tearing at her: Rick. Karl. Kyle. Her father. Gloval. And the fate of all the innocent people on the SDF-1 . . . The cruel faces of the UEDC councilors.

And, more than anything, what she should *do* about it all, because Lisa Hayes wasn't anybody's crybaby.

But she spent most of the time thinking about Rick's frightened voice as the missiles closed in. There's been no word yet of any sightings by the air-sea rescue teams.

In the end it was Rick's voice she heard over and over, Rick's face she saw. Then for a while she did cry, wondering if she would go insane.

"I didn't know! I just didn't know," she wept. Didn't know she would be putting him in danger with the missiles, didn't know how deeply it would affect her and how much she felt for him.

Didn't know if she could go on, if he were dead.

She gazed up to where the bulkhead met the overhead. "Please, *please* don't let him die!"

The Barracuda helo swept in low. The pilot radioed back to the search plane, "Uh, roger, two-niner-niner. I have the dye marker in sight and now have the chute in sight. But I have no movement, I say again, no movement."

The helo descended, churning up the water with the backwash of the rotors. The buoyant VT parachute was below it, lying like a dead sea nettle amid the yellow stain of the dye marker that had automatically been released by the wearer's safety harness on impact with the water.

There was a figure in a flight suit, buoyed by automatic floatation pockets that had expanded when he'd hit, his helmet having sealed itself to keep him from drowning. But all the automatic gear was worthless if he'd been shot while in his ship or coming down.

Big, sinuous shapes were circling; large dorsal fins cut the water. The rescue teams got ready for a pickup while the door gunners did a bit of shark hunting.

Back at the hospital in Macross City, Rick was taken into the ER, priority. The medical personnel continued fighting their *own* battle long after the killing had stopped.

CHAPTER
NINETEEN

It was very strange. It took such an awful mishap to crystallize something that had been so murky up until then. I'm not much for romantic fiction or tell-all autobiographies, but from what I'd read, it's usually something grand and poetic that brings on a realization like this, not just almost causing somebody's death.

Lisa Hayes, Recollections

HE LAY COVERED BY A PROTECTIVE MED-BUBBLE, attached to banks of intensive care machinery.

The monitor-robot overseeing his millisecond-to-millisecond care recorded:

"Lt. Rick Hunter. Multiple lacerations, concussion and minor skull fractures causing temporary encephalographic irregularities. No internal damage. This unit will continue to monitor. Probable symptoms of delirium."

Somewhere deep in his thoughts the word registered, echoing. *Delirium . . . delirium . . .*

He was off on a midnight roller coaster ride, composed of the various wonderful and dreadful experiences he had had in wild juxtaposition throughout the Robotech War.

* * *

He was watching Minmei sing at the Star Bowl, staring at her wistfully. Then an enormous blue-gray hand reached out of infinite distance and grabbed her away. Breetai laughed against a field of stars. "You'll never get away!"

Rick went after them in his VT, through battle and dogfight, only to be chided by Lisa Hayes, only to crash in Macross again. He relived episodes of his time aboard the SDF-1, while Minmei cried out for rescue. Basic training, friction with Lisa, ratracing against pods and a maelstrom of emotions.

He and Max and Lisa and Ben were on Breetai's ship again. And at last he flew his VT to where Breetai sat in the rubble of Macross City, holding Minmei in the palm of his hand like a trained nightingale.

But she spurned Rick's rescue, because, "Lynn-Kyle told me I can't go out with soldiers." And then it wasn't Breetai holding her but a Lynn-Kyle big as Breetai and wearing the Zentraedi's uniform and metal skullplate and crystal eyepiece.

But Kyle self-destructed, and Rick was saving Minmei again in the fist of his Guardian, as he had the first day they'd met.

"Observation hour ten," the monitoring robby recorded. "Lt. Hunter still unconscious. Low-grade fever. Encephalogram remains disturbed."

Rick and Minmei were stranded inside the SDF-1 once more. They stood looking out at the endless Zentraedi fleet, and suddenly it was Lisa standing next to him, then Minmei again. The time stretched out to years.

The Miss Macross pageant and photographers were all mixed into their solitary time together somehow.

* * *

"Patient progressing steadily," the robby told itself. "Prognosis good. Anticipated return to consciousness in approximately one hour."

Rick and Minmei went through their pretend wedding once more. But as he kissed her, Dolza came crashing through the bulkhead, and suddenly Rick was standing beside Lisa on the football field–size table in Zentraedi HQ.

"You shall never have Minmei!" Dolza promised.

"You belong to my world now, Rick; you belong to the service," Lisa told him gently, with love in her eyes.

Then it all dissolved into white light for what seemed like a half second. But when he opened his eyes, he was lying in a hospital bed.

Rick sat up, groaning and dizzy. "What a terrible dream that was," he slurred.

Terrible, yes, in parts, it occurred to him, as the dream fragments blurred even as he sat trying to gather them into memory. But some were wonderful, sending emotional surges through him.

And some had just plain shocked him.

The nurse was taking his pulse to verify what the instruments had told her, which made Rick wonder why they bothered with the instruments.

He groaned, bored stiff, and wondered when they would let him get back on active duty; he had the *flight surgeons* to worry about in addition to the attending physicians.

That was assuming, of course, that fighter ops and Gloval would entrust another VT to a pilot who'd managed to stumble into a barrage of his own side's missiles and get shot down by them.

"Oh, brother; what an *ace,*" he muttered, thinking

that a slightly different pronunciation of the word might be more appropriate.

"Hmm?" asked the nurse. She was young and attractive, with nice legs displayed by the daring hemline of her uniform.

But somehow he wasn't interested. "Nothing. Will I live?"

She dropped his hand and checked his chart. "Basically, you've got a bad bump on the canopy, flyboy. I think you'd better plan on being our guest for a while, Lieutenant, at least until we get the results of your tests back from the lab."

"How come?"

She made a wry face. "So the doctors can find out if it's really true that pilots' heads are made out of granite."

"Why aren't you telling jokes for the USO?"

She patted his shoulder. "Cheer up, Lieutenant. You'll be out of here before you know it."

She turned to go, and he looked out the window at Macross's beautiful EVE sky. "I've got rounds to do," she said. She opened the door. "See you later."

He didn't hear the door close. It took him a moment to realize that he wasn't alone. "Well, look who's here."

Lisa stood in the open door, looking down at her feet. Then she looked up at him miserably.

"Hey, why the long face? Didja come to bury Caesar?"

"Hello, Rick." She walked to his bedside, a small bouquet dangling from her hand. He had a flashback of her face from his delirium but pushed it out of his mind. "I came to apolo—to say I'm sorry," she confessed.

"Apologize? Apologize for *what*, for Pete's sake?"

She turned to put the flowers in a little vase, arranging them so that she wouldn't have to meet his stare. "For your being here. We both know it's my fault that your VT was downed and you were injured."

He couldn't believe what he'd just heard from the ever-in-control Commander Hayes. "Lisa, I have nobody to blame but myself. I made a mistake in judgment and that's *it*, see?"

She brought the flowers to his nightstand. "Thanks for your generosity."

He snorted, "What's happened to that old command confidence? This isn't like you at all."

He still sees me as just a martinet, an old lifer! She went to crumple up the wrapping paper angrily and toss it out. "No, Lieutenant, I don't suppose it is, at that! Anyway—I've said what I came to say, and now I have to get back to my duties on the bridge. Get well."

"Thanks, Lisa. Drop by again?"

As she closed the door: "I don't think so, Lieutenant. I'll be too busy."

On the bridge, Claudia stopped trying to pretend she was taking care of minor duties and turned to where Lisa stood with head bowed over her console, lost in thought.

"How *is* Lieutenant Hunter, Lisa?" Lisa turned around, startled and downcast. Claudia sympathized. "Come on, baby; it can't be as bad as all that."

"You're wrong."

Claudia held folded hands to her bosom. "'And now the sting of Cupid's arrow strikes home!'"

Lisa's mouth dropped open. *"What?"*

"You needn't be ashamed to talk about it, Lisa. I know what it's like to be in love, y' know. Roy and I started out the same way."

"But you two love each other!"

Claudia put her hands on hips. "Of course, silly. So what's the difference?"

Lisa was practically gnawing her fingertips. "I don't think Rick cares."

Claudia leaned close, towering over her. "It's very simple, Lisa. If you're in love with him, go after him! You're in love with Rick Hunter, isn't that true?"

She sighed, nodding slightly. "What should I do, Claudia?"

"Be a woman! Stop moping and—" She gave Lisa a light cuff on the shoulder. "Smile more often!"

The hatch had slid open, and Gloval was on the bridge. "Let me know as soon as logisitics has loaded all supplies."

The two women saluted. "It's already been ordered, Captain," Claudia replied.

He studied the two women, so vital to the survival of the SDF-1. "Is there anything else I should know?"

"No, sir," Claudia said blithely. "I was updating Commander Hayes on other military procedures just now."

"Umm." Gloval stroked his dark mustache. "Well, it's unlikely we'll need much hand-to-hand combat expertise up here on the bridge, but carry on."

He turned to go, and Claudia slipped Lisa a wink.

Rick was listening to Minmei singing on the radio, alternatively recalling shards of his dreams and putting them out of his mind, when the door opened and uniforms started pouring through.

"Hi there, buddy. How goes it?"

Roy Fokker grinned, Max and Ben bringing up the rear. "Big Brother!" Rick said happily, sitting up in bed.

"Y' just can't keep outta trouble, can you? Here." He tossed Rick a gift-wrapped package that was just about the right size for a new robe he had no use for.

Ben cocked an ear to the little radio. "Hey, it's Minmei! That's great!" He fiddled with the volume control.

"Aw, can it, Dixon." Rick slapped the thing off.

Ben stood looking bewildered and hurt. "Whatsa matter?"

"I just like it quiet, all right?"

Ben wore his bemused, goodnatured look, scratching a hairstyle that resemble a fuzzy brown turnip. "Absolutely! Anything you say, skipper! You're the boss!"

"So tell me something, y' big loafer," Roy intervened. "When're you gonna quit playing invalid?"

"'Playing' isn't the right word, Roy."

Max grinned. "What you need is a visit from someone like Minmei, to come over and give you a command performance right here."

Rick turned on him so angrily that Max clapped a hand over his own mouth. Then Rick leaned back on his mound of pillows, head resting on hands. "I don't imagine Minmei's very interested in a washout like me."

Ben sounded his heartiest. "Well, then maybe you oughta introduce her to a certified flying ace like myself, Lieutenant." He laughed loudly.

Rick sat up again, fist clenched. "How about a punch in the nose?"

Roy was on his feet, one hand on Ben's shoulder. To Rick, he said, "Easy, tiger; Ben didn't mean anything."

Big as Ben was, Roy lifted him onto tiptoes without much trouble. "Let's go, ace, before you make his condition any worse."

As he dragged Ben off, Roy threw back, "Glad to see you're okay, kid!"

Max asked Rick, "*Has* Minmei been here? I thought the flowers—"

"No; they're from Commander Hayes."

As Roy paused to open the door, Ben got out, "So what's wrong with that?"

Roy caught his arm. "I said c'mon!"

Ben got off a salute and a "See ya later!" before Roy yanked him out of sight.

"Well, it was nice of *her* to bring flowers, wasn't it?" Max persisted. "Uh, skipper?" Rick wasn't listening, arms folded and chin sunk on chest.

Max saluted uncertainly. "Well, get well soon, sir. Be seein' ya."

Out in the street, Roy told Ben and Max, "At this rate he'll be laid up for months. Guess I'll have to do something to get Little Brother out of this depression."

Ben wore an even more baffled look than usual. "But how, Commander?"

Roy wore a rakish smile. "There's only one kind of medicine that I can think of that'll cheer him up."

Variations, his favorite coffee shop, was fairly busy for that time of day, and so Claudia had a little trouble finding him.

She gave him her bright, winsome smile as she joined him at a window table for two. "Hi, hon; what's the urgent summons all about?" She leaned closer to breathe, "Official business or personal?"

He showed a roguish smile. "A little of both."

She looked him over. "This Minmei business you mentioned *better* be the official part."

"Yep. I have a friend who could use some cheering up; I need to talk to her."

She considered that. "Easy enough; she's making a motion picture. You'll find her on the set every day. *Now*, could we get to the personal part, Commander Fokker?"

He leered at her fondly. "How personal d' you wanna get?"

"Dinner tonight?"

He was coming to his feet. "You got it, kid, but only if you make your famous pineapple salad. But I've gotta get going. See you about seven, okay?"

She watched him rush off again. The SDF-1's new predicament—the work to reequip and rearm combat units, train replacements, restock all supplies, do all maintenance and repair work possible—still left them little time together.

Sure, Commander Fokker, she thought calculatingly. *Dinner tonight and, although you may not know it yet, breakfast tomorrow.*

CHAPTER
TWENTY

So Sammie gave me this puzzled look and said, "But we know perfectly well how bad things look, Claudia. But that's exactly the time when we should go into town and have fun! Didn't you know that?"

All I could do was explain that us old folks are often forgetful and send the Terrible Trio on their way. Whatever they have, there're times when I could sure use some.

Lt. Claudia Grant, in a letter to Lt. Commdr. Roy Fokker

BRON, KONDA, AND RICO LOOKED DOWN AT THE street-corner huckster's portable table, transfixed by fear, awe, and the deeper impulses that their sojourns among the Micronians had awakened.

"Not available in any store!" the huckster ran through his spiel. "Dancing and singing just like the real thing! Batteries not included. Wouldn't you love to have a Minmei doll of your very own?"

Bron, hands clasped reverently, nodded furiously, proclaiming, "I'd *love* to have one of my very own!"

He was squatting now, eyes level with the table, as were his companions. The little mechanical dolls in their bright crimson and gold mandarin robes, black hair bunned and braided like Miss Macross's, didn't actually dance; their movements were more like penguins'. But that didn't stop the gathered children and adolescents from scooping them up.

The huckster, a black-bearded, bald-headed, burly fellow, was doing a land-office business. Nobody even wanted to *look* at bare-chested swordsman dolls or lovable stuffed cutsies anymore. The girls wanted Minmei, the boys wanted mecha—although sometimes it was just the opposite.

"It must be Robotechnology!" Rico muttered to his companions. And a secret weapon, too, he suspected, from its hypnotic effect on him.

The spies had a hopeless long-distance crush on Minmei and an all-consuming yearning to have one of the dolls. But money was still a problem, as it had been since the beginning of their mission.

"We must seize one of them," Konda decided. "On my signal—*now*!"

They came surging up, upsetting the table and knocking the huckster back off balance as he squawked, "Hey, watch it! Ahh!"

The crowd milled, and shoved; Minmei dolls slid or were lofted all over the place as the huckster landed on his rear.

"Grab it!" Konda yelled, and Rico got his hands on one, taking it quickly but lovingly. The fearless espionage agents made their escape in the confusion, clutching their critical item of enemy technology. They could hear the huckster swearing that somebody would be made to pay.

They didn't return directly to the hideout they'd established, of course; that would have been poor tactics. They had to make sure they weren't being pursued.

They couldn't risk having their refuge compromised; it was filled with critical pieces of human instrumentation, things that would give Commander in Chief Dolza and the other Zentraedi lords vital intelligence data and perhaps the key to overcoming the Micronians. There was a piano, an assortment of movie posters, a box of kitchen utensils, radios, TVs and personal computers, a food processor, a bicycle wheel, several street signs, a Miss Macross jigsaw puzzle, and a jumble of broken toys from the city's charity discard bins that the spies so loved.

Every time they thought about their plunder, the spies' chests swelled with pride. But *this*! A Minmei doll! A crowning achievement!

The Terrible Trio paced through the streets of Macross City in the throes of a real crisis.

Kim groused, "will you *look* at us? Walking around town with a day off and nothing to do? No place to go? Ugh, how *boring*!"

"*Ew*," Vannessa agreed.

"*Yuck*," Sammie concurred.

To top it all off, they were dressed for a real good time: Vanessa wore white slacks and a Gigiwear sport coat with the sleeves shot back, Sammie was in a prim but cute outfit that looked like she belonged in the Easter parade, and Kim wore a revealing citypants outfit set off by saddle shoes and knee socks.

"And not a man in sight!" Sammie piped up. "It's a lot worse than just *boring*!"

An abrupt commotion off to one side drew their attention. With pounding feet, three figures came dashing, just about *tumbling*, around the corner. There were three guys, a big husky one and a tall lean one and a small, wiry one, panting and frantic. They crowded on top of one another as they hid around the corner, looking back the way they'd come.

The three spies had recently plugged the special Protoculture chip given them by Breetai into an unguarded portion of the SDF-1's systemry. The towering commander had made it clear that the chip was valuable, irreplaceable, one of a very limited number remaining from the research of Zor himself. The chip would slowly draw on surrounding components and the ship's power to create a pod for their escape. Exedore had been loath to spend the irreplaceable chip even on so important a mission, but Breetai had decided that the spies' return must be assured. And so, they must be sure they weren't pursued.

"Anyone following us, Bron?" the little one said between gulps of air.

"What's the merchant doing?" the tall, lean one panted.

Gasping for breath, the husky one said, "He seems to be sitting there, trying to get the other dolls back."

Rico turned, gloating over their prize, holding the little toy up to inspect it gleefully. "Look: *Minmei*!" The other two bent near, feasting their eyes on it. "Ah!" exclaimed Rico. "Robotech—Robo—uhhh."

He'd noticed something; when Bron and Konda looked up, they too saw three young Micronian females standing nearby, studying them strangely.

Rico was the one among them with a certain presence of mind. He stood up at once, whisking the doll behind his back, sweating profusely. "Um, hello! W-w-we're *strolling*!" The other two nodded diligently in agreement, showing their teeth in unconvincing smiles.

Sammie pointed at them and declared. "Yeah? It looks to me like you're playing with a Minmei doll!"

"D-d-dunno what you mean!" Rico insisted. But the three spies were terrified that their valiant mission had run its course, defeated by the malevolent Micronian genius for war and intrigue.

Sammie shrugged. "It's just that I've never seen a grown man playing with a doll before."

"Adults don't do it?" Bron burst out, trading astounded looks with his cohorts.

Sammie sniggered. "Silly man! Only kids play with dolls."

The spies reflected on the perversely complicated, often contradictory behavioral code the Micronians maintained—no doubt as a safeguard against infiltration by outsiders. A matter of warped genius, and now it had worked; they had blundered and come to the attention of what appeared to be three patrolling secret police.

Vanessa resettled her glasses and took a closer look at the three nerds she and her friends had stumbled across. "What planet d' you come from, anyway?"

Bron went, "Duh," and almost fainted. Konda blurted, "We come from right around here!" and Rico did the best he could, although he was sure they were about to be apprehended and tortured. "Yeah, we work right across the street." He'd heard somebody say it a day or two before, and it seemed to be some kind of verification or identity-establishing phrase.

The spies had learned about "work," a noncombat function considered demeaning and suitable only for slaves among the Zentraedi yet somehow desirable and even *admirable* among the deviate Micronians.

The Terrible Trio looked where he was pointing. It was one of the loudest, most garish spots in Macross City, ablaze with lights and raucous music. The sign over it said, DISCO BAMBOO HOUSE.

Kim clapped her hands. "You mean you work at the disco? We go to the Bamboo House all the time!"

Sammie gave them an even closer look. "I wonder why we've never seen any of you there?"

Bron began, "Uh, what is a dis—" before Rico got an elbow into his middle and he subsided.

Sammie grabbed Rico's wrist. These three guys might be slightly strange, but what the heck? Weird as they were, they worked at the disco, and that would at least mean that they could dance.

"I've got an idea," she said, batting her eyelashes. "Why don't we all check it out together?"

"What a wonderful idea!" Kim threw a fist in the air in elation.

Vanessa figured it was better than another few hours of trudging around town. "I want the big, handsome one," she said, winking at Bron. All the color left his face, and his knees knocked.

Sammie was towing Rico into the street; he didn't dare to resist too much or put up a fight.

"Come with me," she pouted.

"Can't we talk this over?" Rico bleated.

Was this as innocent as the females were making it out to be, or were they superlatively well trained counterespionage agents with a clever plan to drive the Zentraedi spies into paranoid madness and thus make them easier to interrogate?

Bron whispered to Konda, "D' you suppose this disco thing is some Micronian method of torture?"

Kim and Vanessa were looking at them expectantly. Konda hissed, "We must perform our duty as Zentraedi!"

Their chins came up, and their mouths became ruled lines; they advanced bravely to endure whatever sadistic, ultimate torment the experience called "disco" might hold in store.

The cruiser that had been completely destroyed was only a minor part of Khyron's titanic flagship, a part that was now slowly being replaced by the organic growth characteristics of Protoculture.

In the command post bubble overlooking the flagship's bridge, Khyron stood alone, raging at the figure on the projecbeam screen. He'd driven out all his subordinates, even the faithful Grel, determined that they would not witness his helpless fury before the mockery of the woman warrior Miriya.

"How *dare* you question my leadership abilities?" he railed at her. "Just who do you think you are?"

She stood projected before him, erect and lithe, a tall woman with a flowing mane of green-black hair. She drew herself up even taller. "I am the backbone of the Quadrono Battalion, and the finest combat pilot in all the Zentraedi forces."

Khryon snarled, "Your ego will one day cause your destruction, Miriya."

One corner of her mouth tugged upward. "Just as *yours* caused you to be defeated by the Micronians yet again and made you an object of ridicule to all those whom you command, Backstabber?"

He pointed a finger at her. "Because you have never faced a capable opponent, you believe you're something special. But take care, little Miriya! For there is one aboard the alien ship whom you cannot best!"

She heard the would-be taunt with calm interest. "So! A superior pilot, a super-ace, aboard the SDF-1? Interesting!"

She smiled just the slightest bit, dimples appearing at the sides of her mouth, giving her a beautifully hungry, dangerously feline look. "I'd like to meet him!"

Huh! Everything's phony! Roy thought, looking around the movie set. Somehow he'd never believed it even though that was what people had always said. But the little *Shao-lin* temple and its shrine and the trees, plants, and grass were all a variety of cunningly fabricated plastic and other synthetics from the ship's protean Robotech minifactories.

People were running around yelling, mostly being rude to one another. You could tell who was more important, because the other person would just have to stand there and take it. Roy heard things that would have started major fistfights in a barracks, differences in rank notwithstanding.

A man he recognized as Vance Hasslewood, Minmei's personal manager and now codirector of her movie, was running around being important. "Let's set up for the next shot!" "Minmei, Kyle: Relax for a few minutes!" "Wardrobe? Listen, sweetie, those blouses are awful!"

Roy tuned him out, strolling around a phony corner and glancing up a phony staircase. "Well, hey!"

Minmei squealed. "Commander Fokker!" and came racing down the steps to him. She wore a Chinese peasant-style tunic and trousers combination, her hair gathered tightly and done up in a long braid in back.

He looked down on her fondly from his rangy height. "How's everybody's favorite recording star?"

She gestured around at the lights and all the other equipment. "Trying to be an actress. I get to play the cute little heroine."

"Sounds like fun," Roy lied; it looked like appalling drudgery, but then, it was probably tolerable to people who couldn't fly.

"Oh, it *is!*" she enthused. "But—where's Rick? Is he hiding?" She glanced around.

"'Fraid Rick couldn't make it this time."

Her hand flew to her mouth. "He's not hurt, is he?"

"Not seriously, but he's gonna have to spend some time in the hopsital, and I thought you might like to stop in and see him."

Roy's voice took on a slightly harder edge. "That is, if you can spare time from all this." He indicated the overturned anthill confusion of the movie set with a disdainful toss of his shaggy blond head. "I'm convinced a visit from you would be worth more than all the medicine in the world."

Minmei had discovered that life on a movie set was a lot less exciting than she'd pictured it—tedious and time-consuming and endlessly repetitive, just the opposite of what she'd envisioned. She still aspired to superstardom, but the movies' hold over her was less now.

Besides, even though she was flighty, she wasn't blind to the things she owed Rick Hunter. The news that he had been wounded brought out the very best in her—so winning that few people could resist it—and perhaps a sense of *real* drama.

"Of *course* I will! If it weren't for Rick Hunter, I wouldn't even be alive!"

Roy gave her a broad conspiratorial smile. "Atta girl!"

"Commander!"

Roy and Minmei turned together to see Lynn-Kyle

striding their way. He glowered at them, an angry young man in a black, white-trimmed jacket and trouser costume. "If you're through wasting Minmei's time, I wonder if we could get back to work?"

Roy took his time staring down his nose at Kyle. He'd heard all the stories about the fight at the White Dragon. He wondered if Kyle had heard the adage that a good big man will beat a good little man every time. . . .

But Roy knew even more about women than he knew about martial arts and, it is a verifiable fact, preferred the former. Kyle was playing the heavy without even being coaxed; let it be so.

"Of course." He smiled blandly at Lynn-Kyle.

A little frown had crossed Minmei's face at her cousin's boorishness. Then Vance Hasslewood was yelling for his stars—the first team, as he called them.

Minmei's mood appeared to brighten; but Roy wasn't sure, and neither was Kyle. She went running toward the set; Kyle spared Roy a steely look and turned to follow.

Roy left the sound stage whistling happily. He was still feeling pretty smug when the com unit in his jeep toned for his attention. "What is it?"

It was Lisa's voice. "Commander Fokker, one enemy ship has broken out of the fleet and is heading this way, closing fast. Two Vermilion Veritechs are on scramble, and Captain Gloval directs you to take command of the flight and intercept."

"Who's on?"

"Sterling and Dixon," Lisa answered. "Captain Kramer will have your Skull Team standing by for backup as needed."

"Good," Roy told her. "If things begin to boil, I always like those Jolly Rogers around."

The EVE system was off, and the distant reaches of the stupendous hold were above him. Roy Fokker roared his jeep down through a quiet Macross, wondering what the fight was going to be like *this* time.

CHAPTER
TWENTY-ONE

There are few more indicative incidents in the Robotech War, from my viewpoint, than this sudden transference of impulse and disobedience from Khyron to Miriya. The evidence of what was happening was all around them, but still the Zentraedi High Command was, in any meaningful sense, blind to it.

Zeitgeist, *Alien Psychology*

"**S**OUND GENERAL QUARTERS," GLOVAL SAID, his calm, level voice enveloping the bridge. "Prepare pin-point defense shields. Tell fighter ops to scramble Vermilions."

The new attack had come, as Gloval had feared, right in the middle of his own *political* offensive—his effort to make an end run around the Council.

If anybody aboard the dimensional fortress was curious about his encrypted "back-channel" calls to unnamed addressees since his return from the Alaskan fiasco and his silence on the issue of the Council's insane mandates, they'd kept it to themselves. Good crew! No one could ask for better.

The single enemy ship was drawing nearer. The exhausted and heroic logistics people, straining to do an impossible job of taking on the endless rations, ordnance, equipment, life support consumables, and the rest, had secured themselves; the ship was battening down.

The turnaround time for a supercarrier in pre–Global Civil War days, included shipyard overhaul and the rest, ran as much as six months; the United States Navy was doing well if it had *half* its carrier groups at sea at any one time. The SDF-1 had had less than a week to lick its wounds, and unless Gloval's plan worked, it would get no more, but be driven out into space once again.

In the Disco Bamboo House, the three spies, sweating and exhausted from a brave effort to keep up with the torturous convolutions the Micronian females called "dancing," were shocked and worried by the sudden alarms but also relieved. The Terrible Trio's endurance on the dance floor was simply not to be believed.

The women dove for their things, about to head for the door. Sammie stopped to pat Rico's cheek. "You have the strangest style I ever saw, but it was fun!"

Vanessa gave Bron a quick hug. "Let's do it again soon, boys!"

And Kim, blowing a kiss to Konda as she and the others hurried to go, yelled, "We really had a good time!"

Standing there and watching them go, Konda said wonderingly, "You know—I did, too."

The other two looked at him for a moment but then nodded in agreement.

Khyron's words had not seared long at Miriya's pride before she'd taken action.

Now, her own attack cruiser threw off the heat of atmospheric entry unfeelingly, and she and her Quadrono stalwarts poised for the moment when they could go hunting.

Indicators signaled *GO*. Encased in their top-heavy-looking powered armor, the Quadronos stepped one after another into the drop bays.

They were released seemingly at random but all in a plan to assume a combat-drop formation, backpack thrusters blaring, forming up for the assault on the SDF-1.

Inside the green-tinted face bowl of her interior suit, the light gave Miriya's complexion a verdant tinge. "I am looking for one particular enemy fighter," she told the massed assault mecha behind her. "He will show himself by superior performance. When he has been identified, you will maintain distance and leave his execution to me, personally! Am I understood?"

That was confirmed all through her mingled force of Quadrono mecha and tri-thrusters. Miriya monitored her powered armor and contemplated her kill.

There were so many things that made this violation of standing orders so irresistible! There was the chance to show up that posturing fool Khyron; the opportunity to meet an enemy worthy of her mettle (for in his taunt, the Backstabber had been right on target—she'd never met an antagonist she regarded as her equal); a way to defy Azonia; a chance to have the Robotech Masters *sing* the name of Miriya; a crack at ending this war once and for all, to her own personal glory; and of course that ultimate thrill, flirting with complete disaster.

Because if she failed—and Miriya never had—then all would probably be taken from her, her life included. But what was any of it for, if not for the risking? She lived for combat and victory. It was as easy to keep bleeding prey from the jaws of a lioness, as it was to protect the foe from Miriya's attack.

This time, the SDF-1 was ready.

Cat crews nosed up VTs in the launch boxes; the flight decks of the dimensional fortress and *Daedalus* and *Prometheus* were cluttered with combat aircraft, looking like toys under a Christmas tree from the lofty height of the bridge. The VTs' wings were at minimum sweep, ready for launch.

Lisa Hayes had already given Ben and Max the go. Lt. Moira Flynn, cat crew officer, pointed to her shooter. A moment later, Max Sterling rode a rocket off a bow catapult at 200 knots, while Ben Dixon "*Yahoooo*ed" off a waist cat a moment later.

Lisa asked over the intercom, "Is Commander Fokker's ship ready for takeoff?"

Claudia left her station—left it entirely!—and strode over to Lisa. "Is *Roy* leading that intercept flight?"

Lisa bit back what she'd been about to say: *You mean he didn't tell you?* "Yes, Claudia."

Roy pulled on his VT helmet—the "thinking cap," as some liked to call it—as his own trusty Skull fighter's forward landing gear was boxed up by the cat crew.

"Good hunting, Commander," Lisa said, her face on his display screen looking as worried and self-contained as ever.

"I'm more interested in hunting for a pineapple salad," he radioed back.

Lisa couldn't quite believe her ears. She tried to get a confirmation on the pineapple salad transmission as Claudia laughed behind her hand and Gloval marveled at the resilience of young people.

Roy, Max, and Ben joined another flight of VTs off *Prometheus*. In command, Roy took them up and up, going ballistic, all of them eager for the dogfight that had been forced upon them.

Roy looked at them, a bit dismayed. None of the VTs had fought with Quadronos on an even footing yet, except for Rick, who hadn't come out of it so well.

But Roy remembered the souped-up Zentraedi better than anyone, and if the SDF-1 was facing a division of them, that was all she wrote. Endgame.

"Dogfight?" muttered Ben. "You Zentraedi ain't hardly been bit yet! Now, it's *lockjaw* time!"

* * *

Now. Where is this great enemy ace that Khyron fears so? mused Miriya as she and the first few of her armored Quadrono deployed under power to engage a slightly lesser number of enemy aircraft.

She howled a Zentraedi word, a Quadrono battle cry that translated as "Smite them from the sky!"

Immediately the Quadrono battle suits began pouring forth a cascade of fire. The Veritechs dove up into it eagerly, dodging and jamming missiles, betting their reflexes against the enemy's.

Roy did a wingover and banked as a Quadrono's red-hot beams ranged past him. Skull leader did a loop that would have torn the wings off any other fighter ever built, then centered the bulky, top-heavy-looking Quadrono in his gunsight reticle, and thumbed the trigger.

He had a lot of bad-tasting memories in his mouth of how an armored bogey just like this one had rousted him and cost him men in the attack near Luna's orbit. A lot of that pain went away as he watched the Quadrono's head module cave in, then be plowed to nothingness by high-density rounds.

The alien mecha fell, leaving a long, curlicuing trail of oily, red-black smoke.

"Scratch one," whispered Roy Fokker to himself, and went looking for scratch two.

They fought their way up above the cloud cover. One Quadrono burst through, pursuing Ben's banking VT; a second followed, folding into some sort of bizarre fetal configuration, only to bring forth a hornet's nest of missiles.

The missiles moved faster than the eye could follow, detectable only by their flaming wakes and corkscrewing trails of smoke. Somehow, though, they weren't fast enough to get Max Sterling; he twisted and rolled his VT through seemingly impossible maneuvers, jamming some of the missiles' guidance systems, getting others to commit fratricide, and just plain outflying the rest.

He was putting his Veritech through mechamorphosis even before the last of them had gone by. Changing to Battloid mode, he leapt down at his attacker like a cross between a sleek, superswift gunship and Sir Lancelot.

Max fired his autocannon, riddling the Quadrono and blowing it to burning shreds that fell almost lazily. He turned just in time to catch a Quadrono that was trying to sneak up on him. The Robotech chain-gun made its howling, buzzsaw sound again, and the alien became nosediving wreckage.

Miriya had seen it all, the blue-trimmed VT's latest victory in its rampage across the sky. No Zentraedi had been able to stand against it; who else could this be but Khyron's vaunted Micronian champion?

She cut in full power, diving at him like a rocket-powered hawk. "Now you die!"

Except dying wasn't on Max Sterling's agenda today. He dodged her first volley and got a few rounds into her armor as she zigzagged past.

Miriya turned and loosed a flight of missiles that arced and looped at the Battloid, leaving ribbons of trail as graceful as the streamers on a maypole. He dodged those, too, while he charged straight at her, firing all the time. An unbelievable piece of flying.

"You devil!" Miriya grated softly, almost fondly, knowing now what a pleasure it was going to be to kill him. The powered armor and the Battloid whirled and pounced, the upper hand changing sides a dozen times in a few seconds. Miriya was astounded; could this Micronian have artificially enhanced reflexes and telepathic powers? That was certainly the way he flew his aircraft.

She went into a ballistic climb, and Max got a sustained burst into the Quadrono's backpack thruster-power unit. Miriya's mecha trailed sparks and flame as it tumbled back down but suddenly straightened out again; she played hurt and turned the tables once more.

Her particle cannon pounded away at the Battloid, knocking it back as several rounds hit home. Max regained stability by shifting back to Veritech mode and taking evasive action to get a little elbow room before going at it again.

Miriya laughed like some wild huntress and pursued him down through the clouds, crying, "You can't dodge forever!"

"That's very odd," Lisa murmured. "Those alien mecha aren't attacking us. In fact, they seem to be holding off, covering the one that engaged Max Sterling."

Claudia nodded. "It seems like the leader, or whoever it is, has a personal vendetta against Max."

"Who can understand the mind of a combat pilot?" Gloval shrugged. "Especially an alien one?"

"There must be *some* reason Max has been singled out."

She was right. "Order the lieutenant to retreat. If they continue to pursue him, it will mean that the target isn't SDF-1."

Max received Roy's order with a good deal of bewilderment. "Retreat? Wa-wait, I don't get it!"

It would not be exactly true to say that he was having a good time, but he was doing what he did best—did better than anyone else alive. Bashful, unassuming Max Sterling could afford to be deferential and mild-mannered on the ground. It was a kind of wide-eyed but honest noblesse oblige, because in aerial combat he lived life at lightspeed and ruled the sky.

"That bandit on your tail is trying too hard," Roy explained. "They want to find out what his game is."

"You got it," Max said amicably. He *thought* there was something different about this one. At any rate, whoever this alien was, he was one hot pilot.

Max shoved his stick into the corner for a pushover and dove for the surface of the ocean. The Quadrono powered armor streaked after.

* * *

Watching the instruments on the dimensional fortress's bridge, Gloval came to his feet. "So, now we know."

Roy's gift box hadn't contained a bathrobe at all but rather his treasured and superb collection of miniature aircraft.

Rick's favorite was also Roy's: a fragile yellow World War I fighter, a German Fokker triplane with black Iron Cross markings, made at the time of that conflict and nearly a century old. "Fokker, Little Brother, that's me!" as Roy liked to say.

The door opened, and Rick looked to it uninterestedly. Then, abruptly, he was sitting bolt upright in bed. "Minmei!"

She was looking very stylish in a long, red suede coat with white fur collar and cuffs and a pair of yellow tinted aviator glasses. "I hope you don't mind; you didn't look like you were sleeping, so . . ."

He hastily put the toys aside as she came over to him. Whatever subtle things the movie makeup and hairstyle people were doing to her looked great. "Nice big room," she said brightly, glancing around. Her eyes fell on the flowers for a moment.

"It's wonderful to see you."

"I must look an absolute mess," she fished a little, "but I came right over from the studio when I heard you were hurt."

"How'd you find out? Not many people know." Casualty figures and many details of the war were still classified.

"Commander Fokker told me. He came by the set this afternoon to visit me." She patted the bed. "D' you mind if I sit down?"

That's another one I owe you, Big Brother! thought Rick.

"Mm, this is nice," Minmei said, stretching out at the

foot of the bed. Her eyes fluttered, and she yawned charmingly, then laid her head on her arm.

"You look tired."

"I'm exhausted, Rick. There just doesn't seem to be enough time in the day to do the things I'm supposed to do now."

"Would you like to just lie there and get some sleep for a little while, Minmei?"

Her eyes were already closed. "That would be wonderful! If I could just stay here ... for a little while ..."

She was asleep in seconds. Watching her, he mused, *I don't understand what's happening to our world, Minmei, or what's going to become of us. But your safety and well-being makes everything worthwhile to me.*

He sat with his knees drawn up under the sheet, arms folded across them and chin resting on his arms, watching her sleep. He couldn't remember the last time he'd felt so happy.

"Let's get on with it!" howled Roy Fokker, putting a final burst into a damaged Quadrono mecha and sending another Zentraedi flier to the great beyond. The skull-and-crossbones VT banked and dove, looking for new quarry in a sky crowded with missile tracks, alien beams and annihilation discs, gatling tracers and explosions.

The enemy leader and Max were still battling it out for the championship, but Roy and the other VT pilots weren't about to let the rest of the invaders hang around like wallflowers. The RDF fliers were ready and willing to fill their dance card.

The Quadronos didn't hesitate, either. And so: the dance of death.

Captain Kramer, Roy's Skull Team second in command, had shown up with reinforcements when it became clear that the single combat between Max and the enemy leader wasn't simply a diversionary tactic.

Now, Roy pulled out of an Immelmann, split S and zapped another Quadrono just as he saw Kramer zoom past with a Zentraedi on his tail. Roy went after to help, but he was too late; the captain's ship was already in flames.

"Kramer, punch out, damn it!" Roy yelled, waxing the one who'd hit Kramer. "You're clear, boy! Punch out!"

Kramer ejected as another Skull pilot called the SDF-1 air-sea rescue. The captain should have left his chute undeployed until he had fallen well out of the dogfight, but it opened for some reason. Roy figured that meant that Kramer had been hit and his ejection seat's automatic systems had taken over.

Roy circled anxiously, determined to make sure none of the invaders took advantage of Kramer's vulnerability. The grizzled captain had been with Skull Team for years, had flown off the old flatdeck *Kenosha* with him in the Global Civil War. Kramer was the oldest VT pilot on the roster, and Roy meant to see that he got older.

The Skull Leader was so intent on watching over his friend that for once he was careless. He didn't realize it until bolts from a Quadrono chest-cannon blew pieces from his plane.

"Ahh," he groaned, with pain like white hot pokers being thrust through him. Ben Dixon came to his rescue and engaged the Zentraedi before it could make another pass, but Roy's VT began losing altitude, trailing smoke.

The dogfight raged away from him like a tornado of combat ships and weapons fire as Kramer's limp form glided peacefully toward the sea.

CHAPTER
TWENTY-TWO

> *There quite simply had never been anything like it, and*
> *veteran fighter pilots who witnessed it shook their heads and*
> *did quite a bit less boasting for a while.*
>
> Zachary Fox, Jr. *VT: the Men and the Mecha*

MAX AND MIRIYA STILL FOUGHT THEIR INCREDI-
ble duel across the sky.

Max had gone back to Battloid mode, and the two
darted and zigzagged like maddened dragonflies. Max
released another flight of missiles that she avoided, then
nearly clipped her with a tracer-bright stream of gatling
rounds.

But she evaded him again. It was the most difficult,
dangerous, exhilarating contest Max had ever been in;
his sense of time had slipped away, and he didn't think of
victory so much as excelling, of outperforming his foe.

For Miriya it was different. Not only had she *not* destroyed the Micronian, she'd come very close to being
killed herself. He was as good as Khyron had said and
better. For the first time, she was beginning to know
what her *own* opponents, her long list of kills, had felt.

Perhaps, as the ancient wisdom goes, there is always someone better than oneself. The thought repelled her and filled her with an angry dread.

She came tearing through a small white puff of cloud to see that the SDF-1 was close by. "His ship!'

She made straight for it at maximum speed. Perhaps in tight quarters with his own unprotected fellow beings all around, he would know a hesitation to shoot, would lose concentration.

It was a deliciously audacious, risky plan; she adored it.

"I won't be able to catch him in time!" Max hollered over the command net, seeing what this brilliant, devious enemy had in mind.

"They're heading this way, Captain—straight for us!" Lisa reported.

"Tell the AA batteries not to fire!" Gloval barked. "Sterling is too close to the enemy! Make sure all hatches are sealed! Double-check that all civilians are in shelters!"

The banshee song of sirens echoed through the stupendous hold that housed Macross City.

Rick looked up from his peaceful contemplation of the sleeping Minmei. He got to his feet, then staggered for a moment as his bandaged head pounded like a bass drum. He had no idea what the procedure was for patients and visitors during an alert.

Minmei hadn't even stirred. Rick found the corridor empty; he didn't know it, but doctors, nurses, and other staff members were busy helping priority patients— newborns, intensive care, and other nonambulatories. He could hear internal hatches booming shut.

Rick looked at Minmei; for the moment she was as safe where she was as anywhere he could think of. He had to find out what was going on. Rick trotted off to find someone, his head punishing him with every step.

* * *

Most of the exterior hatches on the SDF-1 were sealed, of course, the ship being at general quarters. But one wasn't: the one through which the air-sea rescue helo had just left to make the pickup on Captain Kramer.

The enormous hatch couldn't be closed quickly, but it was more than half closed already. Miriya saw it and dove through it, into the dimensional fortress.

"This is it!" Max steeled himself and followed grimly, his ship in Fighter mode. His rear stabilizers barely cleared the descending upper half of the hatch; the VT's gleaming belly nearly scraped the lower.

He chased the giant powered armor suit through a long curve of enormous passageway usually used to shuttle large machinery, components, and vehicles to and from the fabrication complex situated near Macross City.

"Run, little man, run," Miriya beckoned, watching him approaching in her rearview screen while simultaneously flying at hair-raising speed through the relatively tight passageway. "And when you catch me, you die."

Rick was gazing out through a permaglass window in the solarium, watching the last few civilians scuttle into shelters, when outside debris began falling from overhead.

An enormous figure dropped to the streets of Macross, making the ship tremble. Rick found himself staring at the back of the Quadrono's head.

They're inside the ship! We're finished! The Quadrono's back thrusters flared, and it went racing down the street, taller than some of the buildings, its backwash nearly knocking out the solarium windows.

Rick had barely regained his balance when another cyclopean form dropped from above. Rick recognized the Battloid's markings as Max Sterling's.

Maybe we're not finished, after all! "Go get 'im Max! Yeah!"

Standing erect like the Quadrono, the Battloid flashed off into the streets of Macross in search of its antagonist.

Miriya wasn't used to such close quarters; though she handled her Quadrono mecha well, she bashed through walls and ripped out overhead signs and fixtures. None of that mattered to her, and it didn't affect the mecha at all.

But Max had the advantage of knowing the streets of the city. Miriya came around a turn to see the Battloid, feet gushing thruster fire, skid to a halt before her.

Several blocks separated them. Max whipped up the long, cigar-shaped gray chain-gun and opened fire from the hip. The hail of massive bullets spattered the Quadrono, holing it in places where its armor was thinnest, driving it back off balance. Do what she might, Miriya couldn't prevent her mecha from being knocked over backward.

The Quadrono heaved itself to its feet again, Miriya caught in a red haze of rage. "You think to do combat with *me*?" she screamed, though he couldn't hear her. "You impudent *fool*!"

No radio reply or translation from Max was needed. The Battloid said it all as it stood waiting, poised, with autocannon ready, allowing her the option. The clearest challenge imaginable.

Her words couldn't dispel the thought that assailed Miriya. *Khyron was right! This Micronian is a* demon *of war!*

"Open the overhead hatch that's nearest to them!" Gloval snapped. "We have to force the alien out of the ship!"

The Quadrono's exterior pickups caught the sound of grinding brute servomotors, and Miriya detected the opening of the hatch above her as she shouldered aside a building, crumbling it to pieces like a plaster model, to get some fighting room.

Her Quadrono fired with the energy weapons built into its giant hands—particle beams and annihilation discs. The Battloid ducked one volley, leapt high on thrusters to elude another.

Then Max started slowly walking his Battloid toward the enemy, still holding his fire until he had a perfect shot, determined that his next burst would end the duel. He was sure the other was enough of a warrior to know just what was happening, a test of nerve and backbone.

How close do we come before we open fire? Who gets rattled and shoots first, afraid to go toe to toe? Afraid to shoot it out point-blank?

It was all so bizarre, so impossibly unlikely, a unique moment in the Robotech War. Max couldn't help feeling like one of the good guys in the Westerns he'd loved so much as a kid. If the Duke could only see this!

The Battloid's footsteps resounded, the autocannon cradled at its side like the Ringo Kid's Winchester. Max was a little too busy to whistle "Do Not Forsake Me, Oh My Darlin'," but he heard it in his head.

Miriya almost fired a dozen times in those moments, but pride kept her from it. If the Micronian had the nerve to close the distance to point-blank—to a distance where they'd almost certainly *both* be killed when the shooting started—then so did Miriya, leader of the Quadrono.

On this, our weddin' day-ayy, went the tune in Max's head.

The Battloid's feet measured off ten yards at a stride; the city blocks between the huge mecha disappeared quickly.

It's not good enough simply to die killing him! Miriya's mind yammered. *He must die knowing that I live!*

Before she could reconsider, the Quadrono's thrusters novaed, and the powered armor rocketed up through the open hatch. She loosed a flock of sizzling missiles, but the pursuing Battloid avoided them and kept coming.

Max mechamorphosed to Veritech mode, chasing her in a ballistic climb. "Turnin' tail, are yuh, pilgrim?"

Then Lisa was saying in his ear, "Return to base, Vermilion Three. You've beaten him."

Not decisively, Max told himself, turning for home. He knew that, and the Zentraedi surely did, too.

Seething, Miriya guided her Quadrono back into the stratosphere. "Miriya will not forget this day, Micronian —and you will pay for it. So I vow!"

Elsewhere, the rest of the VTs were chasing the last of the surviving pursuit ships and Quadronos. Roy, fighting down the pain in his chest, managed to drawl, "Awright, Looks like they've had enough."

"Commander Fokker," Lisa said, "you're losing altitude. Are you all right?"

He smiled into the visual pickup and did his best to sound amused. "Yeah, I'm great. But how 'bout Max?"

"He's fine, Commander."

"And my old buddy Kramer? Any word?"

Lisa's face on the display screen was sphinxlike, unrevealing. "He's in intensive care now, Roy. Come on home."

"Roger, SDF-1; we're comin' in."

"Godspeed."

The dreams had been lovely, but the waking was not.

"Ah, so *here* you are! I been lookin' all over for ya! C'*mon*, Minmei! Wake up! Wake up!"

She didn't want to; she'd always loved to sleep. It was so wonderful and cozy, and her dreams were her very best friends.

Now, though, waking up was easier than being shaken so rudely—almost roughly.

She rubbed her eyes, blinking, and looked up at Vance Hasslewood. "What's the matter?"

He made a big production of his exasperation. "*Sweetie, honey*, you're holding up production, that's what's the matter! You're the star! Without you, they can't finish the picture!"

She yawned, looking around, then stopped suddenly. "Wasn't there a young man in here when you came in the room?"

"Hey! Toots! Are you nuts?" He was yelling now; time was money, and when it came to money, Vance Hasslewood could be very unpleasant. His contract said that he got a percentage of every dollar saved if the picture came in under budget.

"You got a *career* to think about, sweetie! Ya don't have time for this kid stuff anymore, *comprende*?" He looked at the bed. It wasn't at all messed up, barely looked slept in. He breathed a sigh of relief; it looked like there'd be nothing to hush up, nobody to bribe, no favors to call in or promise.

"We have five more setups today!" he snapped. "C'mon, babe; let's go." He grabbed her wrist and dragged her off the bed.

Minmei surrendered and trotted along dutifully. She'd discovered that being a star meant that she had to put up with being herded around. She loved the glamour, but she had never counted on having to be so *passive*. Still, it was worth it, she guessed—wasn't it?

"My dad was right," Vance Hasslewood steamed. "I shoulda been a CPA!"

In the Veritech hangar bays, the maintenance crews were getting to work on the parked aircraft. There had been plenty of damage in the dustup with the Quadronos; nobody on the crews was going to be sleeping very much for the next few days.

Two enlisted ratings had deployed the boarding ladder of Skull Leader's ship, ready to climb up to the cockpit. "Whew! This time he *really* got himself clobbered," one said. "I don't believe he could *taxi* this thing, let alone fly it."

He followed his sectionmate up the ladder, bumping into him when the other stopped short. "Hey, what—"

He swung around and came up the side of the ladder

with angled feet, a common practice. And he, too, stopped short when he got a look at the cockpit.

There were bulges in the pilot seat's chickenplate armor and several holes in the back of it. And the seat was red with blood that was now seeping through, running to the floor.

Roy Fokker sat in triage with the others who had been injured. The boys who were really bad had been taken to the ERs first.

Roy had lost a lot of blood, making him light-headed; but the wounds had been closed easily enough, and he was hooked up to a plasma bottle.

"Hey," he asked a passing nurse, "is all this really necessary?" He held up his shunted arm, the plasma tube dangling from it.

"Just shut up and sit there or I'll get Big Bruno the odorly orderly to come sit on that pretty blond head," she said sweetly. She was the same nurse who had looked after Rick, having been mobilized as soon as the alert sounded as part of the special shock-trauma-burn military medical team.

"Doctor Hassan wants a few pictures of your gorgeous insides, dreamboat, to make sure there's no internal hemorrhaging."

Beside being a top-notch RN, she was handsome and leggy and had a way of getting men, even headstrong fighter jocks, to do what she told them. She was an esteemed member of the MM team.

Roy smiled and relaxed, leaning back. She blew him a kiss and went on her way. He felt a little floaty from blood loss, but he'd refused a shot for the pain, so he was lucid.

Then he remembered Kramer. He reached out almost blindly for the nearest institutional-green uniform. "Hey, nurse—"

But he'd grabbed the trouser leg of Dr. Hassan, the

stocky heart and soul of the MM unit. Hassan, a surgical mask around his neck, stopped and looked Roy over.

The doctor and the Skull Team leader knew each other somewhat; Roy had had plenty of his men racked up, had been in that same room quite a few times before.

"Kramer?" Roy asked hopefully.

Hassan had almost been out of the medical profession, maintaining a limited practice, doing some consulting and a bit of teaching, for years up until the SDF-1 spacefolded. Time and events had thrust him back into the center of things, and there was no more dedicated individual on the ship. He had originally started easing out of medicine because of moments like this, and these days such moments were all too common.

"I'm sorry, Roy. He was dead before the rescue people even got to him."

Roy squeezed his eyes shut tightly, tears finding their way out the sides, nodding. He forced his fingers to open, to release the leg of the doctor's trousers. But how do you let go of the pain of a close friend's death?

Hassan patted his shoulder. "Take it easy; I want to take a better look at you. Be back in a minute."

Hassan hadn't gone ten feet when an orderly came rushing up to drag him away for an emergency. The nurse was busy with a stat case that had just come in, another downed flier, this one brought in alive by air-sea rescue.

Unnoticed, Roy disconnected the plasma tube, closing the shunt. His flying suit had been mostly cut off him by the medics, but his robe would do until he could get a uniform. All he wanted now was to be with Claudia—to hold her and tell her he loved her and hear that she loved him.

CHAPTER
TWENTY-THREE

These mecha that they're always talking about—those are a perfect symbol of the warmakers. Our lives and the life of our planet are too precious to be entrusted to the military machines!

All they care about are their battles, their glory, their victories. The only thing they love is their endless killing. They want to control us all to make sure that their war goes on and on until they've destroyed the universe.

And I say, we're not going to let them run our lives anymore. Peace, no matter what the price! Peace now!

From Lynn-Kyle's pamphlet,
Let the People Make the Peace!

CLAUDIA ADORED ROY WITH ALL HER HEART, BUT honestly, sometimes she had difficulty dealing with their love affair—dealing with *him.*

Like now. There he sat on her couch, silent and lost in thought, strumming her guitar softly, his long fingers sure and gentle on the strings. As if he were mute. She made final preparations, the pineapple salad looking magazine-cover perfect.

"All right," she said. "I blew up at Lisa for not telling me you were leading the Vermilions today, but that's squared away between her and me. But what about *you* and me, Roy? It's just not fair to blame me for worrying about you!"

Roy didn't say anything, sitting and strumming. He looked pale and a bit dazed. She made up her mind that he *was* having breakfast with her, and dinner again tomorrow night. She was going to get him to rest even if she had to strong-arm the flight surgeons into taking him off the duty roster!

She turned to look at him from the tiny kitchenette. "I don't think you realize how terrified I get every time you fly off on a combat mission. It's almost as if you pilots think it's all some kind of wonderful game that you're playing when you go up in those Veritechs!"

The music stopped. "It has never been a game, Claudia," he said quietly. "You know that." He wanted to resume his song, to feel connected to the music and to feel connected to Claudia and to feel connected to life.

But his vision was going dim, and he couldn't recall what he'd been playing. He felt cold, unutterably cold.

"Anyway, I said what I had on my mind, and I promise that I'll keep my mouth shut about it in the future," she said, putting a few final flourishes on the halved pineapple.

Claudia told herself to let it drop. They were together, and they would be together that night. She thought of his touch, how tender and caring he could be, how he had always been there whenever she really needed him. And all the other problems vanished; their love had a way of making that happen.

Claudia turned, holding up the salad plate triumphantly. "Well! Don't tell me I put you to sleep!"

His head lay bent back at an awkward angle, the blond hair hanging from it. His hands had fallen from the guitar, and his eyes were closed. He moaned very faintly.

Something about it filled her with a fear worse than anything she'd ever felt on the SDF-1's bridge. "Roy?"

He moaned again, louder, tried to stand up but instead fell, to stretch out facedown on her carpet. The back of his uniform jacket was sodden with blood.

* * *

Roy heard Claudia, far away, and wanted to answer but couldn't. He didn't know how he'd forgotten, but there was a mission he had to fly.

There was Kramer now, with the ships waiting to go. Strangest fightercraft Roy had ever seen: far sleeker and more dazzling than Veritechs, and they seemed to shine with an inner light.

But—how had Pop Hunter, Rick's dad and Roy's old mentor, gotten tapped for this mission?

It didn't matter. There were plenty of good men on this one, many of the best Roy had ever flown with. Why hadn't he seen them lately? Not important. Pop Hunter handed Roy his helmet, and Kramer slapped his back in welcome.

Then they were airborne, going ballistic into the blue, free and proud as eagles. What was the mission, again? Oh, yeah; the big one! How could *that* have slipped his mind?

They were going to ride forth and rid the universe of war itself, so that there would be peace, nothing but peace, forever. Then, after this last mission, he could go home and turn in his helmet and never fly another.

He could hold Claudia to him and never let her go.

The fighters climbed, and the sky became lighter instead of darker, and then impossibly bright. With his squadron arrayed behind him, Roy Fokker zoomed straight into the center of the white light.

"I'm terribly sorry, Lieutenant Grant," Doctor Hassan was saying. "We did everything we could for him. But there was massive internal hemorrhaging, and—he had just lost too much blood."

Claudia was shaking her head slowly; she heard the words, understood what they meant, but they made no sense to her. She was looking down at Roy's unmoving body, not believing he was dead.

Hassan and the nurse looked at each other. The doctor had seen this before; he tried to get through to Claudia again.

"It's a terrible tragedy." He gave the nurse a look; she understood the signal, and they turned to leave Claudia for a while so that she could begin the long, painful healing.

"Commander Fokker will be sorely missed," Hassan said, closing the door gently behind him.

Claudia stared down at Roy's face until the tears blinded her, then threw herself to her knees, burying her face in the sheet that covered his chest.

She wept until she thought her heart would burst, unable to believe he was gone. It seemed that the entire world had simply vanished, leaving nothing but a cold, silent void.

Rick was sitting up in bed, playing with the triplane again, fairly happy, although he didn't realize it. Even worry, lovesickness, and depression couldn't be on the job all day and all night, so his natural resilience had surfaced. He looked up as the door opened.

"Well, hi, Lisa! What's got you out around town on this fine morning?"

Then he saw something in her expression, and all the ebullience went out of him.

Lisa had never been good at this sort of thing; she still didn't understand why she had agreed to be the one to tell Rick.

"Commander Fokker's dead. From wounds suffered during the air battle yesterday."

The little yellow airplane with the Iron Cross markings fell from his limp grasp. "Fokker, Little Brother, that's me!" It hit the floor and broke into a dozen pieces.

"My Big Brother's dead?" He whispered it without tone, with barely the inflection to make it a question, staring at the wall.

When he began weeping into the bunched sheet that he gripped in his fists, racked by sobs that it seemed would tear him apart, Lisa turned to go. But she reconsidered, her guardedness and reserve and the hurt of what she'd taken earlier as his rebuff dropping from her. She went to sit by his side, her arm around him, as he cried inconsolably.

Gloval showed no emotion when he read the casualty report. But he was distant and distracted, remembering the gangling, blond-haired teenager who had flown for him off the *Kenosha*, who had helped him explore the just-crashed SDF-1 when it first came to Earth . . . who had believed so much that war must end that he was willing to fight for it.

Let him be the last! Gloval thought wrathfully. *They're not sending us out for more killing and dying! If I have to end the Robotech War here on Earth, then I will!*

The following chapter is a sneak preview of *Battlehymn*—Book IV in the continuing sage of ROBOTECH!!

CHAPTER
ONE

As far as I'm concerned [Gloval] has already disobeyed his orders; I'd urge the Council to proceed with a court martial if I could only come up with someone to replace him. What do you think, [name withheld], perhaps I could talk [Admiral] Hayes into accepting the position and kill two birds with one stone? . . . This issue of the civilians aboard the SDF-1 has turned into a real mess. Personally, I consider them expendable—along with Gloval, along with the whole ship, if you want to know the truth. Let's face facts: The thing has already outlived its purpose. You and I are where we wanted to be. Why not give the aliens their damn ship and send them back where they belong?

Senator Russo, personal correspondence
(source withheld)

T HERE WAS SOMETHING NEW IN THE COOL SUMMER night skies of 2012 . . . You remember sitting on the backyard swing, hands tightly gripping the galvanized chains, slender arms extended and head tossed all the way back, gazing up into the immeasurable depths of that black magic, teasing your young mind with half-understood riddles of space and time. All of a sudden, your gaze found movement there where none should have existed, as if an entire constellation had uprooted and launched itself on an impromptu journey across the cosmos. Your heart was beating fast, but your eyes continued to track that mystery's swift passage toward the distant horizon, even though you were watching it upside down now and in danger of toppling backward off the swing. A screen door slammed, its report a signal that your cries had been heard, your father and his friends beside you trying to follow the rapid flow of your words, your shaking forefinger, pointing to unmoving starfields. "Past your bedtime," your father said, and off you went. But you crept down the wide carpeted staircase later on, silently, invisibly, and heard them in the library talking in low tones, using words you couldn't fully comprehend in a way that proved you weren't imagining things. You'd glimpsed the fortress, a heavenly city returned from the past, massive enough to occultate the stars... savior or harbinger of dark prophecies, your father's friends couldn't decide which, but *a sign of the times* in either case. Like blue moons, unexplained disappearances, rumors of giants that were on their way to get you... And on the front page of the following day's newspaper you saw what the night had kept from you: a mile-high roboid figure, propelled by unknown devices twice its own height above a stunned city, erect, legs straight, arms bent at the elbow, held out like those of a holy man or magician in a calming gesture of peace or surrender. It reminded you of something at the edge of memory, an image you wouldn't summon forth until much later, when fire rained from the sky, your night world annihilated by light...

In direct violation of United Earth Defense Council dictates, Captain Gloval had ordered the SDF-1 airborne. It was not the first time he had challenged the wisdom of the Council, nor would it be the last.

The dimensional fortress had remained at its landing site in the Pacific for three long months like an infant in a wading pool, the supercarriers *Daedalus* and *Prometheus* that were her arms positioned out front like toys in the ocean waves. And indeed, Gloval often felt as though his superiors on the Council had been treating him like a child since the fortress's return to Earth. Two years of being chased through the solar system by a race of alien giants, only to be made to feel like unwanted relatives who had simply dropped in for a visit. Gloval had a full understanding of the Council's decisions from a military point of view, but those men who sat in judgment were overlooking one important element—or, as Gloval had put it to them, 56,000 important elements: the one-time residents of Macross Island who were onboard his ship. Circumstance had forced them to actively participate in this running space battle with the Zentraedi, but there was no reason now for their continued presence; they had become unwilling players in a game of global politics that was likely to have a tragic end.

There had already been more than 20,000 deaths; how many were required to convince the Council to accede to his demands that the civilians be allowed to disembark?

The Council's reasoning was far from specious, it was crazed, rooted in events that transpired years before, but worse still, rooted in a mentality Gloval had hoped he had seen the last of. Even now the commander found that he could still embrace some of the arguments put forth in those earlier times—the belief that it was prudent to keep secret from the masses any knowledge of an impending alien attack. Secrecy had surrounded reconstruction of the dimensional fortress and the development of Robotech weaponry, the transfigurable Veritech fighters and the Spartans and Gladiators. This was the "logic of disinformation": There was a guiding purpose behind it. But the Council's current stance betrayed an inhumanity Gloval hadn't believed possible. To explain away the disappearance of the 75,000 people of Macross, the military had announced that shortly after the initial-liftoff the SDF-1, a volcanic eruption on the order of Krakatoa had completely destroyed the island. To further complicate matters, GIN, the Global Intelligence Network, spread rumors to the effect that in reality a guerrilla force had invaded the island and detonated a thermonuclear device. *Global Times Magazine* was then coerced into publishing equally unreal investigative coverage of a supposed cover-up by GIN, according to which the actual cause of the deaths on Macross was disease.

Just how any of these stories could have functioned to *alleviate* worldwide panic was beyond Gloval; the Council might just as easily have released the truth: that an experiment in hyperspace relocation had inadvertently ended with the dematerialization of the island. As it stood, however, the Council was locked into its own lies: 75,000 killed by a volcanic explosion/guerrilla invasion/virus. Therefore, these thousands could not be allowed to "reappear"—return from the dead was an issue the Council was not ready to deal with.

The 56,000 survivors had to remain virtual prisoners aboard the SDF-1.

And if the Robotech Defense Forces should win this war against the Zentraedi? Gloval had asked the Council. What then? How was the Council going to deal with the victorious return of the SDF-1 *and* the return of the dead? Couldn't they see how misguided they were?

Of course, it was a rhetorical question.

Gloval's real concern was that the Council didn't consider victory an acceptable scenario.

Which is why he had taken it upon himself to launch the SDF-1. He was going to focus attention on the civilians one way or another . . .

There was panic on the ground and panic in the voice of the Aeronautics Command controller.

"N.A.C. ground control to SDF-1 bridge: Come in immediately . . . N.A.C. ground control to SDF-1 bridge: Come in immediately, over!"

On the bridge of the dimensional fortress there were suppressed grins of satisfaction. Captain Gloval put a match to his pipe, disregarding Sammie's reminders. He let a minute pass, then signaled Claudia from the command chair to respond to the incoming transmission.

"SDF-1 bridge to N.A.C. ground control, I have Captain Gloval. Go ahead, over."

Gloval drew at his pipe and blew a cloud toward the overhead monitors. He could just imagine the scene below: the eyes of Los Angeles riveted on his sky spectacle. He had ordered Lang and astrogation to utilize the newly revamped antigrav generators to secure and maintain a low-level fly-by, so the enormous triple ports of the foot thrusters were scarcely a mile above the streets. There would be no mistaking this for some Hollywood stunt. And not only were people getting their first look at the airborne SDF-1, but also of the formerly top-secret mecha that flew along with her—fighters, Guardians, and Battloids hovering and circling a mile-high bipedal Robotechnological marvel. Forget the majestic colors of those sunset clouds, Gloval wanted to tell them. Here was something really worth photographing!

"Captain Gloval, low flights over population centers have been strictly prohibited except in extreme emergencies."

Gloval reached forward and picked up the handset. "This *is* an emergency. We must maintain a low-altitude holding pattern. Our gravity control system is not perfected, and the lives of our 56,000 civilian detainees are in jeopardy."

Lisa Hayes turned from her station to throw him a conspiratorial wink.

"But sir, you're causing a panic down here. Increase your altitude and fly out over the ocean immediately. It's imperative."

I have them where I want them! Gloval said to himself.

"I will comply with your order if you can give me permission to disembark these civilians."

The speakers went silent; when the controller returned, there was incredulity and urgency in his voice.

"Sir, that's impossible. Orders from UEDC headquarters state that *no one* is to leave your ship. We have no authority to countermand those orders. You must leave this area at once."

It was time to let some of the anger show. Gloval shouted, "I will not rest until those orders are changed!"

He slammed the handset back into its cradle and leaned back into the chair. Vanessa had swiveled from her screen to study him; he knew what was on her mind and granted her the liberty to speak freely.

"Sir, isn't it dangerous to be making threats while we're on the aircom net?"

Claudia exchanged looks with Gloval and spoke for him.

"This fortress is a symbol of the Council's strength," she told Vanessa. "If it gets out that the captain is resisting orders, the Council would lose face—"

"And there's a chance," Lisa added, "that our communication *was* being monitored." She turned to Gloval. "Isn't that true, Captain?"

Gloval left the chair and walked forward to the curved bay. The cityscape was spread out beneath the ship; Veritechs flew in formation, and great swirls and billows of lavender and orange sunset clouds filled the sky.

"I'm prepared to keep the SDF-1 here until we *are* monitored, Lisa." He turned to face Claudia and the others. "I don't think there's much chance that the Council will reverse its decision. But politicians can sometimes be helpful, and it's possible that someone in the government will get wind of this, see an opportunity, and step in."

"But the Council isn't going to like your tactics, sir," said Vanessa.

Gloval turned back to the bay.

"Even if I face prosecution, this is something I must do. Civilians have no place onboard this ship. No place in this war."

But for the time being the SDF-1 was stuck with its civilians. However, it had been outfitted with a reworked shield system. Dr. Lang had dismantled the pin-point barrier and liberated the lambent energy which animated it—the same energy which had materialized with the disappearance of the spacefold generators some time ago. His team of Robotechnicians had then reanalyzed that alien fire, careful to avoid past mistakes, tamed and cajoled it, and fashioned a newly designed harness for it. Where the former system relied on manually operated maneuverable photon discs that were capable of covering only specific portions of the fortress (hence the name "pin-point" system), the reworked design was omnidirectional, allowing for full coverage. It did share some of the weaknesses of its prototype, though, in that activation of the system drained energy from the weapons systems, and full coverage was severely time-limited.

If only the personnel of the fortress could have been similarly outfitted . . . but who has yet designed a shield system for the heart, a protective barrier, pin-point or otherwise, for the human soul?

Roy Fokker was dead.

The VT pilots of Skull Team had their own way of dealing with combat deaths: The slain pilot simply never was. Men from Vermilion or Indigo might approach them in Barracks C or belowdecks in the *Prometheus* and say: "Sorry to hear about Roy," or "Heard that Roy tuned out." And they would look them square in the eye or turn to one of their Skull teammates and ask flatly, "Roy who?" They might press them, thinking they were kidding with them, but the response remained the same: "Roy who?" Nobody broke the pact, nobody spoke of Roy, then or now. Roy simply never was.

Except in the privacy of their quarters or the no-man's-land of their tortured memories and dreams. Then a man could let loose and wail or rage or throw out the same questions humankind has been asking since that first murder, the first death at the hands of another, the one that set the pattern for all that followed.

Perhaps that shell game the Skull Team played with death had found its way to the bridge, or maybe it was just that Fokker's death was too painful to discuss—the first one that hit home—but in any case no one brought it up. Claudia and Rick were each separately cocooned in sorrow no one saw fit to disturb. Kim and Sammie talked about how sorry they felt for Claudia, knowing how much she missed Fokker, knowing that underneath that brave front she was torn up. But neither woman ever approached her with those feelings. Even Lisa seemed at a loss. That afternoon she had followed Claudia to the mess hall, hesitant at the door, as if afraid to intrude on her friend's grief... Did it occur to her that Claudia and Rick—the lieutenant at the observation deck rail and Claudia seated not fifteen feet away—might have been able to help each other through it, or was Lisa also one of the speechless walking wounded, wounds in her own heart reopened, wounds that had been on the mend until Fokker's death?

It was Rick she approached that afternoon, the City of Angels spread out below the observation deck like some Robotech circuit board. Rick looked drawn and pale, re-cuperating but still weak from his own brush with death wounds he had suffered indirectly *at her own hand*. But there was no mention of Roy, although it was plain enough to read in his dark eyes the devastation he felt. And the more she listened to him, the deeper she looked into those eyes, the more fearful she became; it was as though all light had left him, as though his words rose from a hollow center, somber and distanced. She wanted to reach out and rescue him from the edge. There was music coming through the PA, a song that had once wel-comed both of them back from a shared trip to that edge.

"That's Minmei, isn't it, Rick? Have you two been seeing each other?"

"Sure," he answered flatly. "I watch her on the wall screen, and she sees me in her dreams."

No help in this direction; Lisa apologized.

Rick turned from her and leaned out over the rail.

"She's been spending a lot of time with her cousin Kyle. You know, family comes first."

"Well I'm glad you're all right, Rick. I was worried about you."

That at least brought him around, but there was no change in tone.

"Yeah, I'm feeling great, Lisa. Just great."

She wanted to start from scratch: *Listen, Rick, I'm sorry about Roy, if I can be any help to you—*

"So I hear we've got a new barrier system," he was saying. "And I guess we need it more than ever, right? I mean, since the Council is refusing to allow the civilians to leave—"

"Rick—"

"—and it isn't likely that the Zentraedi are going to call off their attacks."

She let him get it all out and let silence act as a buffer.

"The Council will rescind their order, Rick. The captain says he'll keep the ship right here until they do."

Rick sneered. "Good. And the sooner it happens, the better. I know we're all anxious to get back into battle."

Rick's eyes burned into hers until she could no longer stand it and looked away. Was he blaming her somehow for Roy's death? Had she suddenly been reduced to some malevolent symbol in his eyes? First Lynn-Kyle and his remarks about the military, and now this... Below she watched traffic move along the grid of city streets; she looked long and hard at the Sierra foothills, as if to remind herself that she was indeed back on Earth, back among the living. But even if the Council had a change of heart, even if her father came to his senses and allowed the civilian detainees to disembark, what would become of the SDF-1 and her crew?

Where and when would they find safe haven?

ABOUT THE AUTHOR

Jack McKinney has been a psychiatric aide, fusion-rock guitarist and session man, worldwide wilderness guide, and "consultant" to the U.S. Military in Southeast Asia (although they had to draft him for that).

His numerous other works of mainstream and science fiction—novels, radio and television scripts—have been written under various pseudonyms.

He resides in Ubud, on the Indonesian island of Bali.

ROBOTECH™
by Jack McKinney

The ROBOTECH™ saga follows the lives and events, battles, victories, and setbacks of this small group of Earth heroes from generation to generation.